CONFECTIONS OF A PARTYGOER

CULINARY CAT COZY MYSTERY

RUTH HARTZLER

Confections of a Partygoer
An Amish Cupcake Cozy Mystery Book 6
Ruth Hartzler
Copyright © 2021 Ruth Hartzler
All Rights Reserved
ISBN 9781922595072

No part of this book may be reproduced in any form or by any electronic or mechanical means, including information storage and retrieval systems, without written permission from the author, except for the use of brief quotations in a book review.

This is a work of fiction. Any resemblance to any person, living or dead, is purely coincidental. The personal names have been invented by the authors, and any likeness to the name of any person, living or dead, is purely coincidental.

CHAPTER 1

I caught a glimpse of myself in the reflection of the wide glass windows. Art exhibition parties were not quite my thing, but my sister, Rebecca, had been asked to cater cupcakes for the event.

And so, I stood in the small kitchen of the sophisticated building, dressed to the nines and feeling entirely out of place. After all, I had been raised Amish, and decades of living in New York with my then-husband had not quite gotten all the Amish out of me.

I spun around to somebody who had called my name. It was Eleanor. "I wish we could have brought Mr. Crumbles to the exhibition," she said wistfully.

Her comment appeared to enrage Matilda. "Have you finally taken leave of your senses, Eleanor? You can't bring a cat to an art exhibition party. Especially not an art exhibition with traps!"

Eleanor pouted. "Why not? I'm sure it would be considered quite avant-garde. At any rate, it would be in Paris," she muttered.

Matilda waved her arms. "We're not in Paris now, in case it escaped your notice, and we're supposed to be helping Rebecca prepare the cupcakes. And what on earth have you done with that plate, Eleanor? The cupcakes were supposed to be arranged in a pretty and tasteful design. Your plate looks as though your goats have done it."

"They're your goats as much as they're my goats," Eleanor snapped.

I thought it time to intervene. "Both plates look lovely," I lied. "At least they look artistic," I added as an afterthought, "and it *is* an art exhibition."

Rebecca had made smaller, mouth-sized portions of cupcakes for the opening, which was named, 'Interactive Palate of Disorder: a Lively Approach to Snares and Deception.'

Rebecca appeared with a waitress and a waiter, who took the plates. Rebecca's eyes followed them.

"Don't worry," I said. "It will all go smoothly. Everybody loves your cupcakes."

Rebecca ran her hand across her eyes. "I haven't been asked to cater for such a big event before. I'm surprised *Englischers* wanted Amish cupcakes."

"They're all quite the thing now," I told her, "and it's so clever how you turn traditional Amish cakes into cupcakes—Whoopie Pie cupcakes, Wet-bottomed Shoo-fly pie cupcakes, Sugar Cream Pie cupcakes." I rattled off a list.

Rebecca simply nodded and continued to look into the room. After an interval, she said, "Everything is done now. All the cakes are plated up. You three go and enjoy yourselves, and I'll stay here in case any problems arise."

I knew no problems would arise, but I also knew Rebecca wouldn't be comfortable mixing with a crowd at a posh art exhibition. I nodded, and the three of us walked out to join the people milling around, eating tiny cupcakes and drinking champagne.

As a waiter wafted past, Eleanor reached for a champagne flute, but Matilda slapped her hand away. "You're a very cheap drunk, Eleanor."

"I am not!" Eleanor countered.

Matilda put her hands on her hips. "How can you say that? Remember what happened in East Berlin in 1962?"

A slow red flush traveled up Eleanor's face. "I thought we were never to speak of that."

Matilda ignored her and turned away to study a painting. "I think this one's been hung upside down by mistake," she said loudly, drawing stares from people standing nearby. "Shouldn't those spikes point upward?"

I turned away to look at the art installation to my right. It was unusual, to say the least. It seemed to represent wire snakes entwined around a plastic dummy figure. A large red sign warned everybody to keep away.

I was still staring at it when Eleanor spoke in my ear. "Hardly interactive when we're not allowed to go near these art installations," she said. "At least everybody likes Rebecca's cupcakes."

I nodded. "Oh yes, of course they do. Rebecca is a wonderful baker."

I looked around the room. It reminded me of one of the many business events my ex-husband had dragged me to over the years, where he would at once abandon me and speak to his colleagues. None of the other women had spoken to me, presumably as they knew Ted was having affairs. That was my best guess, at any rate. Maybe they were embarrassed to speak to me—who would know?

This space was as I imagined a high-end art gallery would be: shiny white walls, highly polished concrete floors with a subtle hint of granite sparkling in them, and huge windows through which could be seen the twinkling lights of the city below. People whispered as they tiptoed around the strange concoctions of wire and gadgetry. The scent of French perfume hung heavily in the air.

I turned my attention back to Matilda and Eleanor. I sensed, rather than saw, them freeze beside me. A nanosecond later, I wondered if I had imagined it, as they went back to chatting happily. I stole a look around the room to pinpoint the cause of their disquiet. Nothing seemed obvious, so maybe I had imagined it, after all. People were strolling around, eating the cupcakes and drinking champagne while admiring the artwork—at a safe distance, of course.

I decided to check on Rebecca and found her seated at a small table in the kitchen, sipping a cup of hot tea. "Your cupcakes are popular," I said.

Rebecca simply nodded. "I'm all right sitting here, Jane. Why don't you go and enjoy yourself?"

"If you're sure."

She shooed me away, and I walked back in the direction of Matilda and Eleanor.

I hadn't quite reached them when one of the guests, a tall man around the age of Matilda and Eleanor, clutched his throat. I thought he was choking, so I ran to him.

As I hurried, I wondered why Matilda and Eleanor hadn't gone to the man's assistance. After all, they were slightly closer to him than I was.

I bent over him. He whispered to me, and then his eyes shut.

I stood up. "I think he's dead," I announced.

CHAPTER 2

*E*veryone stood, frozen to the spot. Strangely, so did Matilda and Eleanor. It wasn't like them to stay away. I wondered why they were keeping their distance.

"Is there a doctor?" I called out.

A woman pushed her way to the front of the crowd. "I'm a doctor." She dropped to one knee and bent over the man.

After bending over the man for some time, the doctor stood up and made circles with her arms. "I believe this is a crime scene. Nobody is to leave the gallery until the police arrive." She pulled her phone from her purse. Before she called 911, she beckoned over the gallery director. "See to it that somebody locks the exits."

Matilda and Eleanor made their way to my side. "Into the kitchen," Matilda whispered in my ear.

Rebecca was standing at the kitchen door, clutching her throat. "That poor man!"

Eleanor comforted her, while Matilda drew me aside. "What did he say to you?"

I shot her a blank look. "Say to me?" I repeated absently.

Matilda gave me a little shake. "I saw him whisper to you," she said urgently. "What did he say?"

"He said just the one word, 'Burned.' At least, that's what I think he said."

It seemed to make sense to Matilda. She nodded. "Okay, you are not to tell anybody what he said. If somebody asks you, you must say his words were unintelligible."

"But the police…" I began to protest, but Matilda held up one hand to forestall me.

"You *cannot* tell anybody what he said. This is a matter of life and death. We'll explain it all when we get home, but for now, act normal and deny he said anything. Can you do that, Jane?"

I nodded.

The doctor was still giving everybody

instructions to stand over on the other side of the room. She beckoned me over. "The police will want to speak with you."

I nodded. I expected that, given I was the one who had gone to the man's aid.

"Did you see anybody near him?" she asked me.

I shook my head. "I only saw that he was agitated. His hands were at his neck, and I thought he'd choked on something."

"Try to recall everything you can, so you can tell the police. It could be important."

"So, it wasn't a heart attack?" I asked her. "You seem fairly certain he was murdered, but he obviously wasn't stabbed or shot."

The doctor looked around her and then bent her head. "Maybe I shouldn't be telling you this, but he had a puncture mark in his neck."

"Do you think he was injected with poison?"

She shrugged. "It certainly looks like a needle mark and one done in a hurry."

"But how could somebody walk past him and inject him in his neck?"

The doctor gestured to the people dressed in black standing with the guests. "I'm not a detective, but it would be a reasonable assumption that the murderer dressed like one of those people and hit the victim with the syringe as he was going past."

I looked at the people in black. One, an elderly man, was clutching his chest and dabbing at his eyes with a white handkerchief. "But surely not many poisons act as fast as that!"

Once more, she shrugged. "I'm not a forensics specialist. I'm in general practice."

She was about to say something else when the detectives arrived. One was Detective Damon McCloud. His eyebrows shot skyward when he saw me. He hurried over to me. "Jane!" he exclaimed. "And now *another* murder?" He shook his head ever so slightly.

The doctor interrupted us. "This lady here was the first to notice the man was in distress," she said. "I'm the doctor who attended."

Damon took her arm and led her aside a little, out of my earshot. I turned to look for Matilda and Eleanor, but they were nowhere to be seen. I was curious about their secret and what it had to do with this poor man.

After an interval, Damon returned to me. He tapped a pen on his notepad. "Jane, tell me everything that happened."

I took a deep breath before launching into my retelling of the events. "Rebecca is catering cupcakes for this event," I told him. "Matilda and Eleanor are here too. They're with Rebecca in the kitchen." He nodded, and I pushed on. "I happened to notice that the man was in distress. He was clutching his throat, and I thought he was choking. I was only a short distance away, but by the time I got to him, he fell down dead. I called out to ask if there was a doctor, and that lady came straight over."

"Were Matilda and Eleanor with you?"

"No!" I said, probably too loudly. "No, they were with the others. They didn't see what happened." I hoped my tone was sufficiently firm.

"And you didn't see anybody with the victim?"

I shook my head. "No, but the doctor said she thought the murderer could have dressed up like one of those people in black over there." I pointed to the people in the crowd who were now being questioned by the other detective.

"Why are they all dressed in black and wearing hoods?" Damon asked.

"I assume it's something to do with the art installations," I said. "You know, part of the event and all."

Damon appeared to be thinking things over. "And you didn't see anybody in black near the victim?"

"I'm a terrible witness," I admitted, "but no, I didn't see anybody in black walking away from him. Not that I was looking, of course. All of my attention was focused on the man. For all I know, five people in black could have been near him, and I wouldn't have noticed. I wasn't actually looking for that, you see."

Damon afforded me a reassuring nod. "Of course not. That's perfectly reasonable. I'll probably have to question you about this again, Jane. If you remember anything else, would you call me?"

"Of course I will."

"And you're certain Matilda and Eleanor didn't see anything?"

"They weren't near the victim," I said. "Can we leave now?"

"Not yet. We'll have to release everybody together. You go to your friends, Jane, and I'll speak with you later." I had only taken about five steps when he called me back. "On second thoughts, I should question Rebecca, Matilda, and

Eleanor now, and then I'll help Detective Green question the others."

My stomach clenched. I had done my best to keep Matilda and Eleanor out of it, but now it was up to them.

Matilda and Eleanor did not look surprised or upset to see Damon, much to my relief.

Damon greeted Rebecca first. "Hello, Rebecca. I hear you're catering at this event?"

Rebecca simply nodded.

"I'm sure you will be able to go home soon, but you'll have to wait until Detective Green and I finish questioning the others." To Matilda and Eleanor, he said, "Where were you when the victim died? Were you in the vicinity?"

Matilda spoke first. "No, Eleanor and I were puzzling over one of the art installations. We heard Jane call out for a doctor, and then we saw the victim on the ground."

Eleanor butted in. "And we didn't want to go to his side, because the doctor pushed through the crowd quite quickly. We didn't want to get in the way."

Damon appeared to be buying their story, but then again, they were very good liars. I would have believed them if I hadn't seen them watching the scene unfold.

What was going on? And how were Matilda and Eleanor involved? I knew I wouldn't get any answers until we got home.

Damon left, presumably to help the other detective question everybody. "There's obviously a murderer out there," I said. "A murderer with a syringe. Shouldn't they search everybody?"

Matilda and Eleanor exchanged glances. "No, the murderer would have gotten rid of the syringe by now," Eleanor said.

Matilda agreed. "There are plenty of trash cans around, and even some of those weird art installations could easily hide a syringe. I wouldn't be surprised if the murderer was dressed in black clothes like those strange figures who have been flitting about all night."

"That's what the doctor said," I told her. "Do you think Damon knows that? Surely, they should pay particular attention to the people dressed in black."

Once more, the sisters disagreed with me. "The murderer has probably dumped those clothes by now, maybe in the bathroom," Matilda told me. "While all the commotion was going on and everybody was looking at the victim, the murderer probably slipped into the bathroom, removed the black clothes, and stashed them somewhere."

Eleanor agreed. "The murderer would have then rejoined the others, and nobody would be any the wiser."

"I know the murderer is out there in the room," I said with a shudder, "but there would have to be over a hundred people. That's a huge number of suspects."

"We'll talk about it later." Matilda shot me a pointed look.

"I'll put my head around the door to see what's happening." I was keen to get home, to get the facts from Matilda and Eleanor.

Rebecca stood up. "I'll make us all a cup of hot tea. There are plenty of cupcakes left over. We might as well eat while we wait."

I thought that was an excellent idea. I stuck my head around the door to see what Damon was doing. Damon must have sensed me doing so, because he turned around. He gave me a little wave, smiled widely, and headed for me.

To my alarm, I saw he was also heading for one of the strangest art installations, one with a tripwire. There was a big red warning sign on it, but Damon was looking at me, not noticing it. I waved my arms and called, "No!"

It was too late.

Damon's foot hit the tripwire hard. He flew into the air and landed on his ankle, his foot taking his full weight. I heard a sickening crack.

CHAPTER 3

"I want to visit Damon in the hospital," I said for the umpteenth time.

"You can't, Jane," Matilda said from the back seat of the car. "We'll explain everything when we get home."

"But we're a long way from home," I protested. "Why can't you explain now?"

Eleanor piped up. "The less said in a non-safe zone, the better. Let's not speak another word until we get home."

I sighed but had to respect their wishes. I was greatly relieved when I finally reached home, my house next to my Amish sister's farm. I parked the car and then hurried to unlock the front door. I switched on the light and turned to give the sisters an expectant look.

To my dismay, they were nowhere to be found. Maybe they were checking on the goats. I strode outside, but there was no sign of them. I threw my arms up to the sky with exasperation before walking back inside. I made my way to the kitchen and switched on the coffee machine. I knew I wasn't going to get any sleep that night anyway, and drinking coffee wouldn't make much difference.

I was about to pour coffee into three cups when Matilda and Eleanor finally appeared.

"Where have you been?" I asked, thoroughly exasperated.

"Checking on the goats," Matilda said with a big wink. "Wait right here, Jane." With that, she vanished.

I thought I would go completely mad if they didn't explain what was going on, and fast. Still, I had no choice but to wait. I went to the fridge and looked for something that was packed with fat and sugar. I needed comfort food at a time like this. Finally, I selected the chocolate caramel cake I had made the previous day, and it had a thick layer of chocolate-caramel frosting.

It seemed an age before Matilda and Eleanor returned, but was probably only a few minutes. Eleanor was clutching some type of electronic device. It took me a moment to realize Matilda was too. Presently, they took their seats at the table. "The house is clean," Matilda said. "No bugs, no listening devices, no cameras, no camera radio waves."

Eleanor let out a long sigh of relief. "Yes, thank goodness for that. We should be able to get a good night's sleep."

I pushed a coffee cup in front of each of them and waved my finger at them. "Now, please explain what's going on. Oh, and don't cut any corners. I need to know everything, *everything*!" A horrible thought suddenly struck me. "You didn't kill that man, did you?"

Both Matilda and Eleanor gasped. "Of course not!" they said in unison. Mr. Crumbles jumped into Eleanor's lap and proceeded to purr loudly.

"He missed me," Eleanor said.

"Out with it!" I stood up and crossed my arms over my chest. "What haven't you told me?"

"Lots of things." Eleanor shot me a wide smile.

I glared at her. "Will *somebody* please tell me what's going on?"

The sisters exchanged glances. "We might as well tell her everything," Eleanor said.

To my relief, Matilda readily agreed.

Eleanor was the first to divulge the information. "We have a past."

"Everybody has a past," Matilda said. "What a silly thing to say, Eleanor!"

Eleanor shot her a smug look. "Fools and children shouldn't comment on things half said," she said smugly. "You didn't let me finish, Matilda. Matilda and I have a past, Jane. We weren't always elderly ladies."

Matilda grunted and rolled her eyes. Eleanor pushed on. "No, we used to work for the government. We were Black Ops."

I gasped. "Black Ops! You can't be serious! You worked for the CIA?"

Both sisters chuckled. "Of course not, Jane," Matilda said with a sigh. "We were MI6."

"You're British? But you sound American."

Matilda made a clucking sound with her tongue. "Yes, because we were spies, Jane dear. We would hardly be good spies if we revealed our true selves, would we? Yes, we worked for MI6 and, in fact, we worked for The Increment."

"The Increment? I've never heard of them."

Matilda massaged her temples. "Of course not, Jane. It *is* a secret organization, after all."

Eleanor appeared exasperated. "You need to explain, Matilda! Jane, The Increment is a group of UKSF operators chosen to work with SIS."

"You've made it perfectly clear, Eleanor." Matilda's tone dripped with sarcasm.

Eleanor beamed at her. "Thanks, Matilda."

I finished my piece of chocolate caramel cake in one gulp and then took a mouthful of coffee to wash it down. "You're telling me you were spies?"

"Yes, that's exactly what we're telling you," Eleanor said. "MI6 field agents, to be precise. We can't tell you the exact nature of what we did, because we signed the Official Secrets Act."

"And we probably shouldn't be telling you this much," Matilda added, "although we're only skimming the surface, aren't we, Eleanor?"

Eleanor nodded vigorously. "Quite so, quite so." She tickled Mr. Crumbles under his chin.

I sat for a moment, silently trying to process the information. I was beginning to get a headache. I cut myself another slice of chocolate caramel cake before adding some more sugar to my coffee. "And I take it you knew the victim?"

Their expressions both fell. "Oh yes, the poor dear man," Eleanor said. "Poor Scarface."

"Scarface?" I said. "Was that his real name?"

Both sisters burst into fits of laughter. "Of course not, Jane," Matilda said. "That was his code name. Our real names aren't Matilda and Eleanor, either. It *is* true that we're sisters. And before you ask us what our real names are, we can't tell you."

"Yes, because of the Official Secrets Act," Eleanor added. "We can't tell you our code names either. That way, if you are tortured, you won't be able to tell anybody."

I jumped to my feet. "Tortured! Do you think I'm going to be tortured?"

Matilda leaned across the table to me. "Of course you won't be tortured, Jane." To Eleanor, she said, "You're scaring the poor girl! We left that world behind us some time ago."

"So did Scarface, and it didn't do him any good," Eleanor pointed out.

I stirred the sugar into my coffee. "I take it Scarface was a spy too?"

"He was our handler," Matilda said. "He was our handler at The Increment. We haven't seen him in years. Oh, that reminds me, Jane. Scarface whispered to you before he died. He said 'Burned'?"

I nodded.

"He didn't say anything else?"

I shook my head. "No."

"Are you certain?"

"Yes, I'm certain. Does that mean anything to you?"

"Yes, it certainly does," Eleanor said. "It means he was made."

I was puzzled. "Made?"

"Yes, that means his identity was compromised," Matilda said patiently. "And if his identity was compromised, then Eleanor and I are in danger of having our identities compromised too."

"Did he go to the art exhibition to warn you?" I got up and looked through the kitchen cupboards for some Advil. I found two empty packets of Advil. I sighed. I was about to give up when I saw an unopened packet at the back of the drawer. I pulled out two and swallowed them with some water. One got caught in the back of my throat, and I coughed horribly for a moment.

When I took my seat again, I asked, "Where were we?"

"You asked if Scarface was there to warn us, and I can only assume so." Matilda nodded to Eleanor, who shrugged.

"I can't see what other reason he had to be there, and I don't believe in coincidences," Eleanor admitted. "Believing in coincidences will get you killed. Maybe he was following us, which is a concern, as we didn't notice him. We must be slipping."

"Scarface was one of the best in the business though," Matilda said.

Eleanor frowned hard. "So were we, and if we didn't notice him following us, we might not have noticed somebody else following us."

I absently wondered how long the Advil would take to work, when something dawned on me. "You two retired years ago. Was Scarface still on active duty?"

They both shook their heads. "I know Scarface retired when we did," Matilda told me. "It was years ago."

"But he was murdered," I protested. "I've been assuming he was murdered because of his spy past, but do you think he was murdered for some other reason?"

"Of course not, dear," Matilda said cheerily.

"Scarface was definitely murdered because of his spy past, as you put it. He was murdered for revenge, and we know precisely who murdered him. And he'll be coming after the two of us next, won't he, Eleanor?"

Eleanor nodded. "The Raven."

CHAPTER 4

I was horrified. "The Raven?" I repeated. "It's obviously another code name. Who is he? An enemy agent?"

"The Raven would have retired years ago," Eleanor said, her tone dismissive.

"He didn't retire by choice, he was incarcerated," Matilda reminded her. "And he held a particular grudge against the two of us, as well as Scarface."

"What did you do to him?" I asked. "Who did he work for?"

"The Russians," Matilda said, at the same time that Eleanor said, "East Berlin."

They looked at each other and shrugged. "He

was a double agent," Matilda added. "He worked for several superpowers. He was supposed to be working for us as well."

"You mean MI6?" I asked.

The sisters nodded. "But he was playing a few sides at the same time," Matilda told me. "We exposed him, the three of us. He was put away for years."

"In prison?"

They looked at each other and chuckled. "It never came to court, if that's what you're thinking," Matilda said. "He was sent to a very unpleasant place, and he escaped decades later."

"Recently?" I guessed.

"About five or so years ago," Matilda said.

"Did MI6 inform you?"

"Goodness gracious me, no." Matilda shook her head hard. "Eleanor and I are completely off the grid these days. No, we've kept an eye on him after all these years. We knew he'd come after us one day."

Eleanor put Mr. Crumbles on the floor and walked over to the cupboard. She filled up his bowl with cat food. "We thought he'd think we were still in England."

"Or in the south of France," Matilda added. "Most ex-field agents end up in the south of France, or the Greek islands, or in a nice spot in South America."

Eleanor agreed. "We thought Pennsylvania would be the last place the Raven would look for us. Unfortunately, he had eyes on Scarface."

I nodded. "And Scarface led him to you two."

"I hope not," Matilda said. "I haven't had time to process the information yet, but so far I conclude that the Raven had been watching Scarface for a while to see if he would, in fact, lead him to us. The fact that he murdered Scarface leads me to think that he wasn't aware Scarface knew where we were."

My head was spinning. "I really don't understand."

"Think of it this way," Eleanor said. "The Raven wanted all three of us dead." She held up three fingers and ticked them off as she spoke. "One, he wanted Scarface dead. Two, he wanted Matilda dead. Three, he wanted me dead. He wouldn't have killed Scarface if he thought there was any chance that Scarface would lead him to us."

I thought it over for a moment. "But that's good, isn't it? That sounds hopeful."

Matilda allowed herself a small nod. "Possibly, but we can't get ahead of ourselves. The Raven was one of the best assassins of his time, and all his time incarcerated would only make him even more angry with us. He was completely unhinged."

"But what if he comes after you? Should we tell Rebecca and Ephraim? They live so close to us." I waved my hand in the general direction of their house.

"Absolutely not!" Matilda slapped a hand on the table, making me jump. "We shouldn't have even told you, Jane. Now, one civilian too many knows about us. If Rebecca and Ephraim knew about any of this, it would put them in danger. The less they know, the better."

"Matilda is right," Eleanor said. "I know you're concerned about your sister, but you can't breathe a word of this to her. And you also can't tell anybody that Scarface mentioned the word, 'Burned' to you."

"Okay, I won't. Matilda already told me that. So, what do you both do now? Lie low and hope the Raven leaves town?"

Matilda appeared horrified. "Of course not, Jane! We will find the Raven and take him down."

I looked at Eleanor, but to my dismay, she was nodding.

"But he was one of the world's best assassins!" I exclaimed. "You said so yourselves."

"We were pretty good ourselves," Matilda said smugly.

Something occurred to me. "Why didn't The Raven recognize you? I mean, how many years ago did he last see you?"

"I think it was not long after the Second World War, wasn't it, Eleanor?"

Eleanor shrugged. "No, Matilda, it was well into the Cold War years, maybe 1970 something." To me, she said, "But he never got a good look at us, and we never got a good look at him. We were field agents, so we always disguised our appearances, you see. And possibly, we look a little older now."

"But didn't you recognize Scarface when you saw him?" I asked them.

They both nodded. "But we worked very closely with Scarface for many years," Matilda told me. "And when we first saw him at the art gallery, he gave us the signal not to approach. We knew something was going down then. We knew he was going to make an approach in his own time."

"I see," I said, but I really didn't. All this spy stuff was way above my pay grade. "But you're really not going after the Raven, are you?"

"We can't allow the Raven to find us before we find him," Matilda said. "He was in the room at the party that night. We need to investigate everyone who was at the party that night."

I interrupted her. "But that would take forever! There would have been over a hundred people at the party."

"No, we only have to investigate people who are over the age of eighty," Matilda said.

"Oh." I felt foolish—that was obvious. "Eleanor, you said you didn't believe in coincidences. Why was Rebecca asked to cater the event? That can't be a coincidence, can it?"

Matilda nodded slowly. "Yes, that was the first thing that occurred to me after Scarface was murdered. It *is* a concern, because there's a chance that the Raven engineered it to get us to the gallery. However, I think it's more likely that Scarface was responsible. Jane, do you have any idea who asked Rebecca to cater cupcakes for the event?"

I shook my head. "No, I'll find out in the morning, right after I find out how Damon is. Damon!" I let out a shriek. I had forgotten about his injury.

I rushed to the living room and picked up my purse where I had dropped it earlier. I grabbed my phone. Damon had texted me some time ago. "Oh no!"

"What is it?"

I spun around. Matilda, Eleanor, and Mr. Crumbles had followed me into the living room. "Damon says his ankle is broken badly, and he has to have surgery in the morning." I trembled.

Matilda shot me a wide smile. "That's wonderful!"

Was I missing something? "Whatever do you mean?" I asked her. I was tired. It had been a long night.

"They won't allow a detective with a broken ankle to work on a case."

I thought about it for a moment. "So, are you saying he'll be safe?"

"That's exactly what I'm saying. This is not a case you would want Damon to be handling. Now, we're going to have to increase security. We already have cameras around, but we're going to have to use some additional equipment."

"And we're going to have to put Billy into the house yard again," Eleanor said. "It is quite tiresome parking at the front gate and walking to the house, but I'll bet even the Raven won't be a match for Billy's horns."

I looked up. I had been texting Damon while the sisters were discussing security measures. "Are we safe staying here? What if the Raven shoots at you with one of those long-distance sniper rifles or whatever they're called?"

"No, he'll want to make it personal," Matilda told me. "We need to start this investigation as soon as possible. We have to get a guest list from somewhere, and then narrow it down to all male persons over the age of eighty. Then we will need to question them one by one."

"But if you question The Raven, then he'll know who you are!" I exclaimed. It certainly didn't sound like a good plan to me.

Eleanor chuckled. "Matilda doesn't mean question him about Scarface's death," she said. "I'm sure Matilda has more subtle methods in mind."

"You can leave it to me." Matilda's tone was grim.

Eleanor bent down to pick up Mr. Crumbles. "Thank goodness his attack training is coming along nicely."

CHAPTER 5

*E*leanor was acting suspiciously. Eleanor never acted suspiciously, I thought as I rubbed my chin. That was Matilda's job. Something wasn't right. My stomach churned.

"Eleanor." I glanced over my shoulder after parking the car at the hospital. "Is everything okay?"

"Yes," Eleanor replied, far too quickly. "I'm just a bit worried."

"Worried?"

"About Damon. Poor man."

"Hmm." I took the keys out of the ignition. Eleanor was wearing a huge coat. She felt the cold easily, that was true, but it wasn't cold enough for her to look like a Russian extra in a Hollywood adaptation of Doctor Zhivago.

Matilda placed a hand on my knee. She had asked to ride in the front passenger seat for once. "What are you thinking about, Jane?" Matilda asked.

"Doctor Zhivago," I said.

Matilda's mouth fell open. "But you kissed Damon."

I was confused. "Er—yes?"

"And you've got a new man already?" Matilda's eyebrows traveled up her forehead.

"No, he's from a movie."

"Oh, so he's a big movie star, is he?" Matilda snapped. She unbuckled her seatbelt and stepped from the car, slamming the door.

I turned to talk to Eleanor, but she'd already stepped from the car too. Why did everything always have to be a fuss? All I'd wanted was to visit Damon in the hospital. Now, Eleanor was acting strangely, and Matilda was furious because she thought I was having a covert relationship with somebody like George Clooney. Me! Date a movie star! I couldn't help but chuckle as I unbuckled my seat belt.

Damon was groggy when we arrived at his

room. By we, I was thinking of Matilda and myself. Eleanor had disappeared. She had insisted she wanted to take some exercise.

"Is this my wife?" Damon said to his nurse when we stepped into his room. His eyes were red, and his foot was held up in some strange contraption.

I blushed, but then I realized he was pointing at Matilda.

Matilda giggled. "Yes," she replied. "I'm your wife."

I rolled my eyes as Matilda sat at his bedside and smoothed down his hair.

"Matilda," I snapped, "I'm going to find Eleanor."

I don't think she heard me. She was too happy to fuss over Damon. I tried not to feel jealous that I wasn't the one smoothing his hair as I stepped into the corridor. These days, hospitals no longer smelled of pine disinfectant, but the hospitals of my childhood had. Hospitals filled me with terror.

I had no idea where Eleanor went, or why she was acting so shady. Then I remembered the big coat, and how it seemed to wiggle. I was no expert on fashion, but I knew coats were not supposed to wiggle. My blood turned cold. Mr. Crumbles!

"Eleanor," I called as loudly as I dared. "Eleanor?"

I found her by the vending machines. She had taken off her coat, but her face was bright red. "I lost Mr. Crumbles," she admitted.

"He was under your coat, wasn't he?"

"He's my protection cat." Eleanor looked over her shoulder. "I need him to guard me."

"What are you talking about?" I asked. "Where is Mr. Crumbles now?"

"He escaped. I didn't mean to let him go, but you know how wiggly he can get when he wants to run away."

"I'll take this wing," I said. "You take the next wing. We need to find him before he causes any more trouble. This is a hospital, Eleanor. We can't have a naughty cat running around the place."

Thankfully, it didn't take me long to find Mr. Crumbles. He was in one of the offices, sitting on the keyboard, looking with fascination as page after page of files shot out of the printer.

"Oh no!" I exclaimed as I lifted Mr. Crumbles off the keyboard.

"Meow," he replied.

"It wasn't the dog," I said, guessing his excuse. Cats always tried to blame the dog, even when there was no dog in sight. "Did you print these all by yourself?"

Mr. Crumbles looked up at me with big innocent eyes, which I took to be a resounding, *Yes*.

"Let's get out of here before we get into any more trouble."

I opened the door and stuck my head out. The corridor was empty, which meant we could make our escape. Mr. Crumbles did make his escape, but not in my arms. He jumped onto the floor and zoomed down the hall, narrowly missing a nurse, who was too busy with her notes to see him.

"Mr. Crumbles," I hissed as I ran after him.

He wasn't in the nurses' lounge, and he wasn't in the family waiting area. I decided to return to Damon's room, just to make sure Matilda wasn't smothering him with too much love, and on the way, I found him.

Mr. Crumbles was sitting on an elderly gentleman's chest, purring.

"Hello?" I said quietly, stepping into the gentleman's room.

"Hello, dear," he replied. "It seems I have an unexpected visitor."

"I'm so sorry. His name is Mr. Crumbles. A friend of mine sneaked him into the hospital."

"There's no need to apologize. I've loved cats ever since I was a little boy. In fact, this photo album is dedicated entirely to cats. Sit down, and I'll show you."

I couldn't refuse. I didn't want the gentlemen to alert the nurses to Mr. Crumbles, and I didn't want him to feel lonely. Hospitals could be intimidating.

"Oh," I said for the eleventh time after seeing yet another cat. "A cat."

"Yes!" the gentleman exclaimed. His name was Frances, and he told me he used to be a detective. He'd worked in Ireland for many years, solving crimes, drinking coffee, being cool. I knew he was cool, because in one of the cat photos, there was a photo of him wearing aviators and a leather jacket. His beard was darker then. He was leaning against a motorcycle, the cat on the bike's bag.

Frances snapped the album shut, "Now, we need to talk business."

"Business?"

"You need to break me out of here, girl. These people are evil. They feed me terrible food and prod me at all hours of the day and night. They won't even let me visit my girlfriend, Hazel, or my other girlfriend, Minnie, or my other girlfriend, Elizabeth."

I was horrified. Maybe it was the medication talking. "How many girlfriends do you have?"

"The ladies love a detective."

I thought about Damon. I sighed. "I mean, sure. You're not wrong there. But I can't break you out. What if you need some type of medication?"

"We all need some type of medication, girl. I want to go to a bar."

"I thought you wanted to visit Hazel, or was it Minnie?"

"They can all meet me at the bar."

"I'm not going to tell some sweet grandmas to meet you, an escaped man, at the bar. I won't be your accomplice." I spoke in soothing tones.

Frances snorted. "Sweet? Grandmas may be all sweetness on the outside, but on the inside, they are straight-up gangsters. Why do you think they keep sewing supplies in biscuit tins? It's to torment their annoying grandchildren."

"Frances," I said, "just because my housemate sneaks cats into the hospital, does not mean I sneak people out."

"Is she cute?"

"His name is Mr. Crumbles."

"Your housemate, girl."

"You are not dating Eleanor. She's a nice lady. She doesn't need to get all caught up in dating a bad boy."

"She sounds like a bad girl, if you ask me," Frances replied. There was a cheeky twinkle in his eye.

"I'm not breaking you out," I said firmly. "But I'll come and visit you again, if you'd like."

"You, my dear, are always welcome."

I smiled, picked up Mr. Crumbles, and fled the room. I decided not to tell either Matilda or Eleanor about my new friend. Instead, I would tell Eleanor to quit sneaking cats into hospitals and Matilda to stop pretending to be people's wives.

I stepped into Damon's room. He was now fast asleep and snoring loudly. "Matilda, what are you doing?"

"I'm knitting my husband a scarf."

"Alejandro? But you said he disappeared in East Berlin decades ago."

"Damon," Matilda corrected me with a laugh. "My new husband, Damon."

I put Mr. Crumbles on a chair and took the knitting needles out of Matilda's hands. "Matilda, stop pretending that you're in love with Damon. We need to find your sister."

"I'll stop pretending I'm in love with Damon," Matilda replied, "when you stop pretending that you're not."

My mouth dropped open. I was about to say more when I heard nurses shouting and hurrying down the hallway outside Damon's room. For a minute, I had the awful image of Eleanor on her back, legs in the air, some sort of dire medical equipment beeping where it had fallen on top of her.

I raced out of Damon's room and followed the chaos. It led me straight back to Frances's room nearby, only now Frances's bed was empty, and his machine was beeping loudly.

"Where did he go?" a nurse asked.

"Look!" Another nurse pointed out of the window. "Isn't that him?"

I raced over to the window alongside the first nurse. The three of us all looked on in horror as Frances ran down the road, his hospital garment open, his bottom exposed for all to see.

"It's not a bad view," a voice said. I jumped.

It was Eleanor. She was pressing her nose against the glass.

"You're in big trouble," I said.

"Why am I in trouble when that man is allowed to run down the street half-naked?" Eleanor asked, her tone indignant.

"He is *not* allowed to run down the street half-naked," I said, "the same way you are *not* allowed to sneak cats into hospitals."

"Mr. Crumbles is not a regular cat. He's an attack cat."

"Either way, he's currently with Matilda. We need to get back to the room."

"What about that man?"

"Oh, I'm sure the hospital will catch him."

"He's not a stray dog."

"Come on." I took Eleanor by the arm.

We returned to Damon's room. He was now awake. That was the good news. The bad news was he still thought Matilda was his wife, and he was holding her hand while she blushed.

"This day cannot end soon enough," I muttered more to myself than to anyone else.

"Who is this?" Damon said.

"Your ex-wife," Matilda said at once. "We don't like her."

"Matilda!"

"What?" she replied. "He gets annoyed if you don't give him a good answer."

"Is this the woman who keyed my car and sold all my clothes on eBay?" Damon said, as he frowned at me.

Matilda nodded. "Absolutely."

"Matilda!" I said again.

"Honestly, Jane, I am simply doing my best," Matilda replied.

She was doing more than that. I collapsed into the chair beside Damon's bed, giving up. I no longer cared if elderly gentlemen fled from hospitals, or one of my housemates sneaked attack cats into places no attack cat had any business being. I wanted to crawl into bed with a good book. I wanted to fall asleep as the rain pitter-pattered on my roof.

Damon shook himself. "Jane?"

I sat up. "Damon? You're okay?"

"You came to visit me." He shot me a wide smile.

I thought he was going to add something romantic, maybe profess his love for me. Instead, he said, "Why is that naked man banging on the window?"

I turned around to see Frances, now

completely nude, giving me the thumbs up. "I'm on the lam," he yelled. "Thanks for your car keys."

"My what?" I said.

He held up the keys in his right hand. The old mischief-maker must have stolen them when he was pretending to show me pictures of his beloved cats.

"Jane," Matilda said, "why did you give that handsome naked man the keys to your car?"

I sighed and slumped back into my chair. "No one speak to me for the next decade," I replied. "Maybe make that the next two decades."

CHAPTER 6

I was tired and stressed by the time I reached Rebecca's cupcake store. There were no customers when I arrived.

Rebecca looked up. "How is Detective McCloud?"

"He's just had surgery on his ankle, but he's not in too much pain," I said. I hoped he wouldn't be in too much pain when the strong painkillers wore off.

"I'm glad it wasn't anything more serious." Rebecca set some sample cupcakes on a tray. "It's been quite busy this morning, but nothing I couldn't handle."

"I'm sorry I wasn't here."

Rebecca waved my apology away. "*Nee*, I'm glad the detective's injuries are not too serious."

"Somebody stole my car."

Rebecca gasped. "What happened?"

I told her all the details, leaving out the part about the lack of clothes. "But Frances didn't get far. He fell asleep a block away. Thankfully, he parked first. The nurses said it was his medication." I walked behind the counter. "Rebecca, who invited you to cater for the party last night?"

"Somebody recommended me to the gallery director," Rebecca said. "I think that's what he said."

"Oh, that's right. I remember you said a man came to speak with you about the cupcakes, and he sampled some."

"*Jah*, that was the gallery director."

That surprised me. "The gallery director himself?"

Rebecca nodded.

At once, my stomach clenched. I tried to recall what the gallery director looked like. I remembered the doctor had called over the gallery director the previous night.

The director had looked about Matilda and

Eleanor's age. A distinguished man, he was tall, slim, with white hair and a white beard. Could the gallery director be the famous double agent himself? And if that were the case, then the gallery director must have been suspicious of Matilda and Eleanor. Why else would Rebecca be selected to cater the cupcakes? I considered cupcakes were not the usual fare for a gallery opening party.

I walked into the back room to fetch a tray of Red Velvet cupcakes and then placed them in a display cabinet. "Rebecca, did the gallery director mention why you were selected to cater for the party?"

Rebecca shrugged. "Not as far as I know. He only said that somebody recommended me."

"And he didn't say who?"

Rebecca shook her head. "No, and I didn't ask." She shot me a long look. "Jane, you're not thinking of investigating, are you?"

Before I could answer, two men in suits walked into the store. It was obvious to me they were detectives, even before they identified themselves. The older one walked over and flashed his badge. "Hello, I'm Detective Tom Williams, and this is Detective Bill Martin. And you are Jane Delight?"

I nodded. "I am."

"Do you mind if I ask you a few questions in private?"

"Sure, come into the kitchen." As I led him into the kitchen, I could hear the other detective questioning Rebecca.

I indicated Detective Williams sit at the small table opposite me.

"I do realize you have given your statement to Detective McCloud, but he's no longer on this case."

I simply nodded. I wondered if the detective knew of my relationship with Damon. If he did, he gave no indication. The detective pushed on. "Would you mind going over it again with me? Tell me the events in as much detail as you can. Please don't leave anything out, even if it seems small and insignificant to you."

"Sure." I absently looked at the oven and took a deep breath before launching into my retelling of the previous night's events. "And then I saw him clutching at his throat. I thought he was choking, so I ran over to him," I concluded.

"Go on," the detective prompted me.

"That was it, really. He fell to the floor, and I could at once see that he was dead. I asked if there was a doctor, and a woman hurried through the crowd to him."

"The doctor was not in the vicinity at the time?"

I shook my head. "No, she seemed to come from the back of the room."

"Who *was* in the vicinity at the time of the victim's demise?"

Matilda and Eleanor were there, but I wasn't about to admit that. "There were several people milling about," I said. "There were several guests and also the gallery staff dressed in those funny black capes and hoods."

The detective scribbled away on his notepad. "Did you see one of the people dressed in black near the victim?"

I rubbed my head hard and then put my head in my hands. I had tried to remember that over and over again. "I don't specifically remember, but I do think I saw someone dressed in black walk away," I told him. "I can't be sure though. I mean, I wouldn't be able to swear to it in court, but I do think I recall that."

I looked at his face to see if he was displeased by my words, but his expression remained impassive.

"And had you spoken to the victim that evening?"

I shook my head. "No, not at all. The first time I noticed him was when I thought he was choking."

The detective nodded. "Could you please show me what he did with his hands?"

"Do you mean you want me to recreate it?"

"Yes, if you would be so kind."

I clutched at my neck, trying as hard as I could to replicate the victim's movements.

"I see. And did you speak with the doctor?"

"Yes, we had a conversation. She said she thought he had been injected with poison because she saw a needle mark."

"Do you remember her exact words?"

"No, I'm sorry."

"Please try."

I did my best to remember and told him as much as I could. That seemed to satisfy him.

"Thank you, Ms. Delight. We will most likely need to question you again."

He stood up.

I stood, too. "Do you think he was actually injected with poison? Or could it have been a heart attack or something like that?"

The detective narrowed his eyes. "I'm afraid I'm not at liberty to divulge that information."

"Of course." I felt foolish for a moment. After all, detectives wouldn't investigate a homicide case if the victim had died of natural causes. But then, I reminded myself that the forensics tests would not be back yet, so the detectives at this point would not know whether it was a homicide or natural causes. One thing was clear—they were certainly already treating it as a homicide. To me, that suggested there had, in fact, been a needle mark in the man's neck.

As I followed the detective back into the storefront, I wondered if the detectives were suspicious of the doctor. Could the Raven have an accomplice? I would have to ask Matilda and Eleanor. The doctor had been bending over Scarface for some time. I was certain she could have surreptitiously injected him with something without anybody else noticing. What if she or the Raven had slipped him a sedative in a drink, and then, later, the doctor had finished him off?

I shook my head. My imagination was running away with me. I realized Rebecca was showing the detectives out of the front door. "What did he ask you?" I asked her.

Rebecca walked back to take a position behind the counter. "Nothing, really. He wanted to know if I saw anything, and I told him I was in the kitchen the whole time."

"You were looking around the door for a while," I reminded her.

"Yes, I told the detective that. He showed me a photo of the victim and asked me if I'd ever seen him before."

"And had you? Had he ever been in the shop?"

Rebecca shrugged. "I told the detective I hadn't seen him before. He certainly didn't look familiar to me."

That was interesting. If Scarface had wanted to warn Matilda and Eleanor, I would have thought he would have gone into Rebecca's store at some point. The store certainly seemed a safer place than a public event to make contact with them. Or maybe he thought a public place was safer.

I was at a loss. The police had no idea this was a matter of espionage, a decades-old revenge murder. Matilda and Eleanor, and possibly, Rebecca, Ephraim, and I were in danger until this murder was solved.

But the murderer was no ordinary citizen—the

murderer had been one of the most dangerous assassins in the world.

I had no idea how I would start investigating this, but one thing was clear, we would all be in danger until the Raven was apprehended.

CHAPTER 7

*I*t was with trepidation I pressed the buzzer at the gallery door. There was a closed sign on the door, but the lights were on inside. I hoped the gallery director was in so I could ask questions, although part of me wished the director wasn't in. I had no wish to engage in a battle of wits with the Raven.

Matilda and Eleanor had warned me to be especially careful. They had instructed me to go there under the pretense I was doing some sleuthing because the police suspected me. My aim was to find out the name of the person who had recommended that Rebecca cater the party.

I saw the shadow of a tall man behind the

glass, moments before the door opened. It was indeed the gallery director.

He pushed his glasses up on his nose. "I'm terribly sorry, I have forgotten your name," he said. "You were with the caterer, the Amish lady, weren't you?"

I took a deep breath and plastered a fake smile on my face. "Yes, I'm Jane Delight," I said brightly. "I'm actually Rebecca's twin sister."

His white, bushy eyebrows shot skyward. "But, but you're not Amish," he sputtered.

"I left the Amish many years ago after my *rumspringa*," I told him. "Would you mind if I asked you a few questions?"

I thought I would have to go into more detail, but he held the door open and beckoned me in. "Please come to my office. I assume this is about that most unpleasant situation last night?"

"Yes, it is indeed," I said. I did my best to tamper my growing apprehension.

He showed me into a large room that stood in stark contrast to the sleek, contemporary art gallery. This room was filled with antiques, not French antiques or quintessentially American antique furniture, but traditional English antiques of the Victorian era, maybe even earlier.

The only modern item I could see in the room was a laptop, but it was sitting on top of a pile of yellowed papers. I wouldn't have been surprised to see a typewriter. Classical music was playing softly, but I couldn't see the source.

"I am Reginald Ramsgate." The elderly gentleman leaned forward and offered me his hand. "You may call me Dr. Ramsgate."

I shook his hand, noting he had a rather firm grip.

"And I'm Jane Delight," I said again.

He sat back and looked at me expectantly.

I launched into my prepared story. "I'm quite concerned because the police suspect me of the murder."

He gasped. "Surely not!"

I nodded and made an effort to look sad. "Yes, simply because I was with that man when he died. It was just a case of wrong place, wrong time, for me, but the police think it was deliberate." I shrugged. "I expect they don't have any other suspects at this point."

Dr. Ramsgate took off his glasses and rubbed them with a polishing cloth before popping them back on the end of his nose. I wondered why he wore glasses, as he looked over the top of them at me. Maybe they were only for reading. "Yes, it's terrible," he said. "They questioned me at length too. Most upsetting."

"I told them I had never met the victim, but I don't think they believed me," I told him. "I don't even know the victim's name."

He nodded slowly.

I thought I might as well press him for answers. If he didn't answer my direct questions, then that would be suspicious. "What *was* the victim's name? I looked on the internet this morning. They mentioned the incident in vague terms, but the news report didn't give any names."

He looked alarmed. "Oh, I see. You're asking me? Oh yes, the poor dear boy. His name was Marvin Maze. He was one of the volunteers here at the art gallery."

I was surprised. "Oh, you knew him! For some reason, I assumed he was a guest who had walked in off the street."

Dr. Ramsgate's eyes glinted. "Why would you assume that?"

I shrugged. "I suppose I hadn't given it any thought really," I said, keeping my tone nonchalant. "It's only after the police visited me in my sister's cake store today that I thought I had better do some sleuthing."

"Aha." He latched his hands together and twiddled his thumbs. "I see. And this is the actual reason you have come here. To ask me questions about Marvin."

I shot him what I hoped was a disarming smile. "Yes, if you don't mind. I don't want to be falsely accused."

"I assume *nobody* wants to be accused, either falsely or otherwise."

I nodded. "That's why I wanted to find out the victim's name and find out something about him. Maybe he had enemies."

"I can't see how Marvin could possibly have had any enemies." Dr. Ramsgate stroked his beard. "He seemed a most affable man."

"Somebody murdered him, so he had at least one enemy."

"You do have a point. Tea?"

I was startled, and said, "Yes, please," automatically.

Dr. Ramsgate left the room, and after about five minutes, returned with a tray. He set the tray on the desk between us and then handed me a dainty porcelain teacup covered with yellow marigolds. "I collect Aynsley porcelain," he said. "Before I was an art director, I collected fine antiques."

"You have some beautiful antiques in the room," I said. Maybe he wasn't so suspicious, after all. "How long have you been the director at this gallery?" I was relieved his words had provided me with the opening to ask such a question in a non-suspicious manner.

He looked away at the ceiling. "Let me see. Around eight to ten years, I might say."

The sharp pangs of anxiety slowly ebbed from my stomach. The Raven escaped from prison five years ago. This man could not be the Raven. There was nothing I could do but push on with my questions. Maybe he would know something. "Did Marvin have any particular friends? Was he close with any of the other volunteers?"

"I don't think so. He seemed to be a loner. In fact, I was surprised to see him at the party."

"How long had he been a volunteer here?"

Once more, Dr. Ramsgate stroked his beard. "Only about three or so months. Or was it five? No, I don't think it was quite five months. I can't be sure."

"Would you have any records?" I could see he was about to protest, so I hurried to add, "I know you have privacy rules, but the poor man is dead, and this knowledge might keep me out of prison. I certainly didn't murder him."

Dr. Ramsgate held up one hand. "You don't need to assure me, Jane. I believe you. All right, I'll look up the records for you, but please, this will have to be our little secret." He winked at me.

I expected him to open the laptop, but he crossed to a filing cabinet on the other side of the room. He pushed aside the wilted leaves of a half-dead potted plant and opened the top drawer. He brought out a beige folder and put it on the table in front of him. On it, scrawled in flowery handwriting, was the word, *Volunteers*. He turned it over and jabbed his finger on one of the papers. "Here he is. Marvin Maze. He started here precisely twelve weeks ago." He looked up at me. "But surely that can't assist you in your investigation?"

I shrugged. "You never know." I drained my cup in one gulp. The tea was lukewarm.

"Would you like another cup of tea?"

"Yes please, but then I must go. I don't want to take up any more of your time."

Dr. Ramsgate hurried to reassure me. "Not at all, not at all. Would you like your tea weaker or stronger?"

"No, it was perfect as it was," I told him.

He picked up my cup and set it on the tray. His hands trembled ever so slightly. I wondered if it was an act. He left the room, and I could hear him in the kitchen.

I pulled my phone out of my purse, raced around to the folder, opened it, and took a photo of Marvin's address. The name directly under Marvin's name was *Silas Greeves*. Next to the name was an asterisk, and scrawled next to it alongside five asterisks were the words, *Requested to be in costume for installation party but I think too feeble*. I took a photo of that too.

I hurried back around the desk and sat back down on my upholstered chair. My heart was beating out of my chest.

I could never be a spy—I was far too nervous for that. I looked at my phone to make sure the writing in the photo was legible, and to my relief, it was. I turned off my phone and shoved it back in my purse.

I was still shaking when Dr. Ramsgate re-entered the room. I hoped he didn't have cameras hidden around the room, but even if he was the Raven and did have cameras in the room, I figured he would simply conclude I was snooping in an effort to clear my name.

I drank the tea, wondering if there were any other questions I could ask him. Only one occurred to me. "The doctor who tried to save Marvin…"

He interrupted me. "Yes, Dr. Smythe. What of her?"

"Do you know her well? Does she come to many of the openings?"

He nodded and smiled, a look of enthusiasm flooding his face. "Oh yes, she is one of our favorite patrons. She buys art from us from time to time."

"Did she buy any art last night?" I didn't particularly want to know—I was simply trying to keep the conversation about the doctor going.

Dr. Ramsgate chuckled. "Art installations are not to her taste, but Dr. Smythe does attend all the openings. She is more of an investor. She likes to buy the works of up-and-coming artists, and on occasion, she sells works on commission through the gallery."

That was when it hit me. I had forgotten to ask

the most important question. "Who recommended my sister as the caterer for last night's party?"

"Oh, it was Marvin. He said he had been to your sister's store many a time, and he assured me the cupcakes were delicious."

That unnerved me. On the one hand, it was clear it was Marvin's way to get Matilda and Eleanor to the party, but on the other hand, the Raven might find Marvin's recommendation suspicious.

Dr. Ramsgate's next words relieved my fears somewhat. "Last month, Marvin recommended another local baker. We liked to choose a different caterer for each monthly event, you see. Spread goodwill around the community and all that."

I had finished my tea, so I set my cup in my saucer. "Thank you, Dr. Ramsgate. You have been most helpful."

Once more, he offered his hand, and I shook it. This time, his grip was nowhere near as firm. I didn't know whether I should read anything into that. "My pleasure, Jane. Now you take care, won't you?"

I walked away, trembling. Despite Dr. Ramsgate saying he had worked there for years, I was troubled—had I been in the presence of the Raven?

CHAPTER 8

I parked the car outside the gate to my house and walked around to fetch some hay for Billy, the attack goat. I spotted Billy hiding behind a tree. At least, his head was behind the tree, but the rest of him was sticking out. I laughed, but I knew I wouldn't be laughing for long if I didn't have a large handful of hay. While Billy was eating hay, he was not his usual vicious self.

"Jane!"

I spun around to see Rebecca walking toward me. "I wanted to speak with you, but I'm not going to walk to your house while that goat is there." Rebecca shot Billy a look.

I laughed. "He's hiding behind that tree, and he thinks we can't see him."

Rebecca pulled a face. "I don't see the funny side of that goat, Jane. Anyway, I wanted to speak with you about Detective McCloud."

I gasped. "Is he all right?"

"*Jah*, as far as I know. I would like to invite him to stay with us until he recovers enough to be on his own."

"That's kind of you," I said.

"He lives by himself, and with a broken leg he won't be able to fend for himself," Rebecca added. "Of course, you could invite him to stay with you, but I knew you wouldn't because it wouldn't be proper with three single women in the house."

"Err, no," I said.

Rebecca was still talking. "Of course, there's a man in my house, Ephraim, so it's entirely appropriate. Are you going to the hospital again this evening, Jane?"

I told her that I was.

"Would you invite him on my behalf?"

"Sure. I'd be happy to. Thanks, Rebecca."

She gave a little wave and then turned back toward her house. I grabbed a big handful of hay and let myself in through the gate.

As soon as I latched the gate behind me, Billy appeared only a few paces from me. It was like a horror movie, or so I imagined. I didn't watch horror movies. They were far too scary for me. I only liked Hallmark movies. I turned my attention back to the goat. I offered Billy the hay, and he wasted no time latching his big, yellow teeth onto it. He pulled with all his might.

I walked backward toward the house, holding the hay out in front of me. "This is ridiculous!" I said aloud. "I'm living with two octogenarian ex-spies. We're all being targeted by one of the world's most famous assassins, and we are relying on an attack goat to protect us."

Billy lowered his head and made a threatening motion with his horns. I at once held the hay closer to him. "Maybe the Raven wouldn't be any match for those horns, after all," I considered aloud.

And would Damon accept Rebecca's invitation? I was almost embarrassed to ask him. At least when I visited him tonight, he wouldn't mistake Matilda for his wife.

I reached the front porch. Matilda flung the door open. "Quick, inside."

I threw the hay at Billy and slipped inside the house. I hurried over to the couch, kicked off my shoes, and threw myself backward. "What a day!" I exclaimed.

Eleanor appeared from nowhere and thrust a cup of meadow tea into my hands. "Tell us everything," she said.

I told them the conversation, word for word. "He said he's been working for the gallery for eight to ten years," I told them. "That would be easy enough to check."

Matilda shook her head. "That doesn't discount him. There are ways around that."

I showed them Scarface's address on my phone.

"I think this Dr. Reginald Ramsgate made it too easy for you to find that address," Eleanor said. "I find it suspicious that he left the folder on the desk and went out to make you another cup of tea."

"But why wouldn't he believe my cover story?" I protested. "If he investigates me, he'll know I've had a hand in solving other murders in recent times. He'll simply think I'm nosy."

"Eleanor's right for once. I don't like it," Matilda said.

"Do you think it's a trap to lure you to that address?" I asked.

They both nodded. "Possibly," Matilda said. "It might be booby-trapped."

I was exasperated. I had thought finding the address was a big plus. "Then what are we going to do?"

"We will have to go and snoop around at that address, nevertheless," Matilda said, her tone firm. "We will just have to give a considerable amount of thought about how we approach it."

"And what of Silas Greeves?" Eleanor asked. "The note says he was too feeble to be in costume."

Matilda interrupted her. "By costume, I assume it means dressed as one of those figures in black."

Eleanor frowned. "Yes, I was getting to that. If this Silas was in costume, then he too is a suspect. I assume he's over eighty."

"Why, because he's described as feeble? Don't be ageist, Eleanor!"

Eleanor rounded on Matilda. "*I* wasn't the one who said he was feeble, Matilda! Dr. Ramsgate did, if indeed it is Dr. Ramsgate's handwriting on the list. Don't shoot the messenger!"

Matilda scowled at her. Nevertheless, she simply said, "We need to question Silas Greeves."

"We need to investigate the doctor too," I told

them. "The more I think about it, the more I think she could have injected Scarface. She told everybody to stand back, and she was huddled over him."

Matilda nodded slowly. "But we do need to get the guest list."

I was remorseful. "I should have asked Dr. Ramsgate for the guest list."

"No matter," Matilda said. "He most likely would have refused to go as far as giving you that, even if he *is* a legitimate gallery director. We'll simply break into the building and retrieve it. Jane, you said the filing cabinet didn't have a lock?"

"That's right," I said. "But we don't know where he keeps the guest list."

"Most likely in the filing cabinet," Matilda said, "but we will have a good look around when we get there."

"And when are you going to do this?"

The sisters looked at me. "Don't you mean *we?*" Matilda said. "The three of us should break in."

"What if somebody is watching the building?"

"We'll go in disguise, of course," Matilda said. "We can hardly break into a building looking like ourselves, can we?"

I was horrified. "What sort of disguise did you have in mind?" I shuddered, having been the victim of one of their hideous disguises in recent times.

"We will have to give it some thought, won't we, Eleanor?"

Eleanor beamed from ear to ear. "Indeed!"

"But if Dr. Ramsgate *is* the Raven, and he becomes aware that three people have broken into his office, he will realize it's the three of us. Three isn't a good number," I said hopefully.

"You leave the breaking-in details to us," Matilda said. "We've had years of experience. Don't you worry about it."

But that's exactly what I was doing—worrying about it. "And when are we going to break and enter?" I asked her.

"There's no time like the present," Matilda said. "We'll go tonight."

"I want to go to the hospital to see how Damon is first."

"Sure," Matilda said. "The timing will work quite nicely. After you visit Damon, we'll put the disguise on you in the car. Eleanor and I will already be in disguise and waiting in the car for you, out of sight."

My imagination ran away with me. I thought of all the horrible disguises they could insist I wear. "Can we at least eat dinner first?" I asked them. "It seems as though it's going to be a long night. A *very* long night."

I remembered that Rebecca wanted me to invite Damon. "I almost forgot. Rebecca wants me to invite Damon to stay with her and Ephraim until he's back on his feet, metaphorically and literally speaking."

Matilda bit her lip. "That's kind of her, but will Damon take her up on her offer? Some men don't like to be fussed over."

"And some men don't like to be away from the Internet," Eleanor said. "I can't see Damon fitting into the Amish way of life, even if it *is* only for a few days. No electricity, no Internet, but then again, Jane, he'll have you nice and close. That might make up for the lack of amenities."

My cheeks burned, and I was certain my face had turned beet red. "Rebecca's cooking is superb," I told them. "That might make up for the lack of Internet. Besides, he'll have his cell phone."

"And you could take him some books," Eleanor said. "I got these out of storage last night. I'm sure he'd find one of these interesting, given his line of work."

I looked at the titles of the books lying on the coffee table. The first was, *Silently Strangling People in Hand-to-Hand Combat: A Guide*. The second was, *Cyanide, Arsenic, Thallium: Old-Fashioned but Useful Ways to Poison a Victim*. The next was, *The Chinese Death Touch: New Trends in Techniques*. I did not want to look at any more.

"I think we should have scrapple for dinner," Matilda said.

Eleanor looked puzzled. "Scrapple?"

Matilda tut-tutted. "Oh, my goodness, Eleanor, you've had scrapple many a time before. It's a mixture of pork scraps, cornmeal, and buckwheat flour."

Eleanor stomped her foot. "I know what scrapple is! We usually have it for breakfast. I just didn't think we had any, that's all."

Matilda rolled her eyes. "Yes, that's because I made it *all by myself*. It's in the refrigerator. I'll heat it up, while you and Jane make a start researching Dr. Ramsgate."

Matilda walked away, muttering to herself, while I went to my bedroom to fetch my laptop.

By the time I returned to the living room,

Eleanor was already tapping away at the keys. "Dr. Ramsgate has a Facebook timeline, but his privacy settings are high."

I sat on the couch and opened my laptop. I found Dr. Ramsgate's Facebook profile within moments. "I'm going to scroll down to see when he opened his account," I said. "Oh look, he's had it for eight years."

Eleanor tapped her chin. "Maybe he murdered the real Dr. Ramsgate and assumed his identity."

I chuckled. "It seems we can discount him."

"Not so fast, Jane." Matilda walked into the room with two steaming plates. She set them on the table and then left. I had to wait until she returned with the third plate, along with a large bowl of applesauce, for her to continue speaking. "The Raven would be able to hack somebody's account easily. For all we know, he started that Facebook page only a few weeks ago."

I thought that over. "Okay then, I'll look for news of the gallery."

"I've already done that," Eleanor said. "Come and see."

Matilda and I looked over her shoulder. Eleanor tapped her index finger on the screen. "This is a news item from four years ago at one of the gallery openings. This is clearly the same man."

Matilda rolled her eyes. "But that doesn't mean anything, Eleanor. We know the Raven escaped four years ago."

"I know that," Eleanor snapped. "That photo was simply for the purposes of comparison." She opened another tab on the computer. "Look here—this is a news article about a gallery opening eight years ago."

I adjusted my reading glasses and peered at the screen. "The image is a bit blurry, but it does look like the same man," I said.

"The Raven is a master of disguise," Matilda countered. "My money is on the man pretending to be Dr. Ramsgate. He murdered the original Dr. Ramsgate and took his identity. It's obvious he picked someone who looked just like him."

Eleanor raised her eyebrows. "*Just* like him? What are the odds?"

It was Matilda's turn to stomp her foot. She certainly was in a mood. "You very well know what I mean, Eleanor. I meant somebody of the same gender, height, age, and weight. He obviously murdered the real Dr. Ramsgate and buried him somewhere, somewhere where he wouldn't be found."

"But what about the dental records?" Eleanor protested.

"Dental records?" Matilda shrieked. "Whatever are you on about, Eleanor?"

"How did Dr. Ramsgate make sure that the body would never be found? He couldn't take that risk, not if he really *is* the Raven. If the real Dr. Ramsgate's body was found, then the game would be up. No, I don't think he could risk it."

"I do take your point, Eleanor," Matilda said, as though she begrudged it, "but that doesn't mean he didn't have a good way of disposing of the body. Maybe he put him through a meat grinder. Maybe he dissolved him in a bath of acid. Maybe…"

"Please stop!" I said. I clamped my hands over my ears. "This is too much! I don't want to hear another word."

"Is there an Egyptology section attached to the art gallery?" Eleanor asked.

Matilda looked at her as though she had gone mad. "An Egyptology section? It's not a museum, Eleanor. It's an art gallery!"

Eleanor looked quite put out. "I just thought that would be a perfect way to hide a body."

"What would?" Matilda asked through clenched teeth. Her cheeks turned beet red. I thought she would explode.

"Why, in a sarcophagus, of course. What if the Raven murdered the original Dr. Ramsgate and made him look like a mummy? Who would ever look in a sarcophagus for a murder victim? I mean, a murder victim less than three thousand years old, of course."

I hurried to change the subject. "Shouldn't we check to see whether Dr. Ramsgate has any living relatives? If he has a child, a sibling, any relative at all, then that person would know he wasn't the real Dr. Ramsgate."

"It would help if his privacy settings on Facebook weren't so high," Eleanor complained.

"We'll have to ask somebody who knows him," I said. "One of the volunteers at the Art Gallery."

"That's a good idea." Matilda afforded me a small nod of approval.

"And speaking with one of the volunteers will give us more information on the suspects in general," Eleanor added. "We need to start with Silas Greeves. But first, we need the list of guests at the event. And we haven't discussed this before, but we also need the list of volunteers."

"That's obvious, Eleanor," Matilda said, her voice filled with disdain. "That is obvious."

"If it was obvious, why didn't you think of it yourself?"

"Obviously, I *did* think of it myself, but it was too obvious to mention."

"Has anybody fed Mr. Crumbles his dinner?" I asked, to forestall the brewing argument.

Both sisters said that they had.

I nodded. "Then let's eat our scrapple because I want to check on Damon before we break into Dr. Ramsgate's office."

Thankfully, the sisters turned to their food.

My stomach churned. I certainly didn't want to break into Dr. Ramsgate's office. What if the police apprehended us? Or what if Dr. Ramsgate was, in fact, the Raven and was waiting for us?

A cold trickle of apprehension ran up my spine.

CHAPTER 9

I was relieved to see Damon sitting up in the hospital bed. Apart from being horribly pale, he looked like his usual self. "Jane!" His face broke into a smile.

I crossed over to him and sat on the hard chair next to the bed. "How are you feeling?"

"Much better, thanks. The nurses told me you had visited earlier."

"You don't remember?"

Damon shook his head. "Apparently, I had a reaction to the medication."

"He's not the only one," said a voice from the doorway.

I turned around to see Frances, now thankfully

fully clothed. He walked into the room and pulled a chair over to the area near Damon's feet. He wasted no time sitting on it. "I told Damon earlier about the reaction I had to my medication." He chuckled.

"Yes, and you stole my car," I admonished him.

Frances continued to laugh. "Sorry about that, but it wasn't me. It was the medication, you see. And there wasn't a scratch on your car, was there?"

"No," I had to admit. I had been hoping for some alone time with Damon, but I could see Frances wasn't going to take the hint and leave us alone.

Frances was still speaking. "And where is that charming young lady you were with earlier?"

"Young lady?" I scratched my head.

"I think he means Matilda." Damon was doing his best not to smile.

"Oh, Matilda?" I nearly slipped up and said she was waiting for me in the car. "She didn't come with me," I said, stating the obvious.

Frances's face fell. "I hope she comes with you again soon."

I turned to Damon. "Damon, Rebecca and Ephraim have asked me to invite you to stay with them until you can move about on your foot."

Damon's ears turned pink. "Oh, that's awfully nice of them, but I couldn't possibly impose."

"Why not?" Frances clamped his hand down on Damon's leg, causing Damon to grunt with pain. "Sorry. But why not? I know we detectives like to be strong, but how will you get about and look after yourself if you can't walk?"

"I'll have crutches," Damon pointed out.

"Don't be a fool, man. Go and stay with these people." Frances turned to me. "These are friends of yours?"

"Rebecca is my twin sister, and Ephraim is her husband. They live on a farm next to my house."

Frances's face broke into a wide smile. "All the better then!" He winked at Damon.

I was horribly embarrassed. I wanted to leave, but I also wanted to spend time with Damon. I thought about calling Matilda to act as a decoy, but she was already in disguise. My spirits fell.

"Please thank Rebecca and Ephraim for me," Damon said.

I looked at him. "But?"

"There is no but."

I did my best not to show my delight. "Does that mean…?"

Damon was now smiling widely. "Yes, I'd love

to take them up on their kind offer, but only for a day or two, mind you. I would have been all right if it had simply been a matter of crutches, but they're releasing me tomorrow, and I still feel strange after the reaction to my medication."

"Don't get me started on reactions to medication," Frances said. "I had the most dreadful reaction. I escaped from the hospital and stole a car."

"I know, it was *my* car," I pointed out. "Damon, what time will they release you tomorrow? If you text me, I'll come and fetch you."

"After the doctor does his rounds," Damon said. "And who knows when that will be?"

Frances agreed. "It could be anytime, really. I'm going to miss you, Damon. I'll miss swapping our detective stories."

A nurse popped her head around the door. "Really, Frances, you only have yourself to blame. You checked yourself in, saying you had broken your foot. We found out nothing was wrong with your foot, and you only had to stay here because you had a bad reaction to the painkillers."

"How is that Frances's fault?" I asked her.

She sighed. "There was obviously nothing wrong with his foot. Oh well, at least Frances was able to keep Detective McCloud company as he arrived soon after the detective." With that, she left.

I stood up. "I had better go. Matilda and Eleanor are waiting for me." That, at least, was the truth. I shot Damon an awkward smile, gave Frances a little wave, and then left the room.

When I reached the car, I slipped into the driver's seat. Matilda at once shooed me out. "You won't be able to change while you're sitting there. There's not enough room. Get into the back seat with Eleanor, and she'll help you."

I did as she asked. Matilda swiveled around. "How's Damon?"

"He's going to take Rebecca up on her offer."

"Of course, he is," Matilda said. "There was never any doubt."

"And Frances was there too."

"So, he's back in the hospital?" Matilda stuck her head around once more. "How was he? How did he look?"

"Fully clothed for once," I told her.

Before Matilda could say any more, Eleanor thrust what looked like a roll of thick bandages at me. "What are those?" I asked her.

"You have to wear bindings to make yourself look like a man."

"Bindings?" I looked at the white bandages.

Eleanor tapped herself on her chest. "For the girls, of course. You have to look flat-chested, like a man. Now, take off your outer garments, and I will bind you."

I cast a look around the parking area, but thankfully no one was in sight. I had parked in the most remote corner I could find. Eleanor wrapped the bandages tightly around me. I winced. "Ouch, that's too tight."

Thankfully, Eleanor didn't take too long, but the whole process was rather painful. She handed me a man's shirt. "And put on this bald cap. You will be wearing a man's wig over it." She stuck a tight cap on my head.

"Why does everything have to be so tight?" I grumbled.

"You might as well stop complaining, Jane, or next you'll complain about the glue," Matilda said.

"Glue?" I asked, just as Eleanor squeezed the contents of a tube around my hairline.

"We can't have the man's wig flying off if there are any cameras trained on you, can we?" Eleanor pulled something else out of her purse and flicked it on before holding it at my head.

"What's that?" I asked in alarm.

"It's part of every good disguise equipment," she said. "A battery-powered hairdryer. We can't wait around all day for this glue to dry." She trained it on my head. Now I was hot and wearing too- tight clothes. This disguise business was no fun at all.

After Eleanor finished gluing the bald cap to my head, she stuck the wig on my head and applied more glue. I opened my mouth to complain and then thought the better of it. There was no point.

After the second lot of glue dried, Eleanor tied a wide band around my head tightly, finishing with a big bow.

"I'll take that bow off when the glue is dry," she said.

I sighed with relief, but my relief was short-lived when Eleanor produced a large bag of stage make-up.

"Now we're going to make you look like an old man too," she said.

They were already in their disguises, and both

looked like old men. "Shouldn't we go in disguise as *young* men?" I asked them. "The Raven knows you're both over eighty, so he would be expecting people over the age of eighty."

"Yes, and that's exactly why we're going to go there looking like people over eighty," Matilda said. "The Raven won't be expecting us to look like we're over eighty. He'll be expecting us to go in disguise."

"But we *are* going in disguise, as old men."

Matilda beamed at me. "Exactly!"

I knew there was no point arguing with them. It didn't make any sense to me, but then again, I had never been an international spy.

I drove away in the direction of the art gallery, but Matilda instructed me to head north-west. "We're taking a taxi," she told me. "Park at the nearest McDonald's. We don't want your car to stand out."

I did as she asked. "Now, I'll call a taxi from the other side of the building," she said. "Jane, try not to draw any attention to yourself. Walk slowly behind us. Oh, and Eleanor, explain how to use the walking stick."

"I know how to use a walking stick," I said. "It doesn't take much imagination."

Eleanor shook her head. "Jane, this is no ordinary walking stick. It's a weapon." She showed me the button on the side, which at first, I thought was a bone insert in the pattern at the top. "Press this twice in quick succession, and a knife will slide out."

I was shocked. "You expect me to stab somebody with a knife?"

"Of course, I don't expect you to stab someone," Eleanor said. "Still, we need to go in armed. I can't give you a demonstration in the car because the space is too confined."

"You should have given her a demonstration at home," Matilda said.

"Maybe *you* should have given her a demonstration at home."

"Come on, Matilda and Eleanor. Let's get this over with. I want to get home and get some sleep tonight." I hoped we would make it home safely and not end up sleeping in a prison cell, or worse.

Soon, the three of us were making our way—slowly—to the other side of the building. Before long, we were in a taxi heading for a bar near the art gallery. Matilda asked the driver to deposit us outside the bar.

I climbed out of the door slowly, following

Matilda and Eleanor's lead. I made to go into the bar, but Matilda put a hand on my arm to restrain me. "We're not going in," she whispered. "The fewer people who see us, the better."

I turned around to see Eleanor making a pretense of tying her shoelaces. When the taxi was out of sight, we walked away. Matilda walked in front of us. I thought we were taking a rather circuitous route to the art gallery. Matilda must have guessed my thoughts, because she whispered, "We're avoiding the cameras in the streets."

Presently, we came to an alley, which Matilda turned into. A high brick wall loomed in front of us. "What do we do now?" I whispered.

"On the other side of that wall is a private courtyard at the art gallery," Matilda told me. "It's the Sculpture Garden."

"That's all well and good," I said. "But how do we get in there?"

Matilda seemed puzzled. "We go straight over that wall, of course."

"But we're not ninjas," I complained. "How on earth will we get over that wall?"

The sisters ignored me, as they were too occupied with throwing their walking sticks over the wall. I followed suit. Matilda cupped her hands, and Eleanor placed her left foot in Matilda's cupped hands. "One, two, three, go," Matilda said.

The next thing I knew, Eleanor was airborne. With the skill of a trained gymnast, she landed on top of the wall and couched like a cat. Mr. Crumbles would have not been able to do better.

"Hurry, Jane, it's your turn," Eleanor called down to me.

"I can't do that!" I protested.

"Just put your foot on my hands," Matilda said. "Come on, Jane, it's just like riding a horse. Pretend the wall is a horse, and I'm giving you a leg up."

Filled with trepidation, I did as she asked. I gingerly stepped onto her cupped hands. The next thing I knew, she had somehow shot me into the air. I bit back a squeal and grabbed the top of the wall with both hands. Eleanor grabbed my right arm. "Quick, shimmy over on top of the wall."

It took me all my strength, and I was certain I had dislodged some of the binding bandages, but after an effort, I managed to get myself onto the top of wall. I would certainly have to do some exercise in the future. I was horribly unfit.

"How will Matilda get up here?" I asked Eleanor.

"Like this," Eleanor said. She balanced herself on the wall, stomach downward, and reached out her hands.

Matilda walked away from the wall for several paces and then turned around. She sprinted at the wall and jumped into the air. Eleanor grabbed her arms and swung her onto the wall.

"Now we jump down," Eleanor told me.

"But it's too far!" I protested. "I'll break something."

"It's not that far," Eleanor said. "Lower yourself down until you're hanging by your fingertips, and then let yourself fall, but make sure you keep your knees bent. Here, I'll show you."

She demonstrated, falling gracefully to the ground. She made it look easy. I did my best, but I landed with a thud. A wave of nausea hit me. "I'm not going back this way," I told them firmly.

"No talking from now on," Matilda said. "And follow me. I know where the cameras are. And keep your walking stick close to you."

"How do you know where the cameras are?" I asked her, but no response was forthcoming.

Matilda put her finger to her lips and simply said, "Shush."

We shimmied around past the wide glass doors and found a small entrance with, 'Private: Staff Only,' written across it in faded yellow lettering.

Matilda did speak then. "I know where the official cameras and alarms are, but if the director is in fact the Raven, then he will have other security measures. I have no idea where those would be. We need to get in and out as fast as we can. When we reach the office, we will go straight to the filing cabinet and get the guest list and the volunteer list. Do not speak. We must try not to interact with each other, and we need to get in and out as fast as we can. Do you understand?"

I nodded.

Matilda used a device to unlock the door and motioned that we should stay outside. She waved another electronic device inside. I assumed she was deactivating the alarms. I certainly hoped so, anyway.

Once inside, Matilda and Eleanor abandoned all pretense of walking like elderly men. I followed their lead. Once more, Matilda did not take the direct route to the office.

The office door was locked, but Matilda had

no trouble opening it. I went straight to the filing cabinet. I reached for it, but Matilda slapped my hand away and shook her head.

Eleanor pulled a device from her slim backpack. I had not noticed the backpack until now. She waved it over the filing cabinet and then gave the thumbs up, before pulling the top drawer open. Matilda shone a flashlight into the filing cabinet.

We at once found what we were after, a file labeled *Volunteers* and a file labeled *Guest List: Art Installation Party* with the date. There were other guest lists from previous art gallery opening parties, but the sisters ignored those.

Eleanor took the file labeled *Volunteers* to the desk, and Matilda took the file labeled *Guest List: Art Installation Party* to the desk. They opened them both and shone their flashlights on them. Matilda gave the thumbs up and crossed back to shut the filing cabinet.

I was relieved, thinking we could leave, so I was horrified when the sisters started snooping around the room. I was under strict instructions not to speak, so all I could do was stand there, anxiety gnawing away at me.

What if we had inadvertently set off an alarm,

and the police would be here at any minute? I could hear sirens in the distance. My heart beat out of my chest. A cold sweat broke out on my forehead. Surely, the sisters had heard the sirens, but they did not appear concerned in the least.

Matilda was looking in drawers and in other filing cabinets, while Eleanor was waving electronic devices around the room.

It seemed like an age before they finished. Matilda gave the signal, and I slipped out the door with Eleanor, hard on her heels. I wasn't pleased to find myself in the courtyard again. I would have to tackle that wall again.

"Isn't there another way out?" I lamented, when the back door was safely shut behind us. At least the sirens had continued past us.

"We need to get out of here and fast," Matilda said. "You got in, Jane, so you can get out."

"But how?"

"We will go in the same order as before." She cupped her hands, and the next thing I knew, Eleanor was sitting on top of the brick wall.

I had no choice but to follow suit. I put my foot on Matilda's hands, and she gave me a hefty boost. This time, Eleanor was reaching for my arms, and I thought I did a little better on this attempt.

Soon, Matilda was sitting on the wall with us. When I hit the ground on the other side of the wall, once more a pang of nausea overwhelmed me. I wondered how the sisters were so fit when they were about twice my age, but then again, they had kept superbly fit all their lives, while I had mostly lived on coffee and chocolate.

CHAPTER 10

We arrived home at some dreadful hour in the early hours of the morning. In fact, I had been so tired I had allowed Matilda to drive.

Matilda always drove horribly fast and took corners sharply, but even that wasn't enough to keep me awake.

Eleanor shook my shoulder. "We're home, Jane."

I tumbled out of the car and then saw we were only at the gate. "Oh no," I moaned. That meant we had to get past Billy, the attack goat.

We each grabbed a handful of hay and let ourselves into the paddock. Billy materialized beside us, his teeth flashing and his mouth open, hopefully for the hay and not for his pound of flesh. I held the hay out beside me and strode toward the house, my bed beckoning to me.

As soon as we were safely inside the house, Matilda and Eleanor told me to stay still while they searched the house.

I was so tired, I leaned against the door. I did my best to keep my eyes from closing because I didn't want to fall asleep and end up on the floor. I don't think I had ever been so tired in my whole life.

Matilda and Eleanor presently emerged. Both were smiling, and I wondered where they got their energy from.

"Coffee," Matilda said rather too brightly. "We'll discuss the case."

I staggered forward. "Can we discuss the case in the morning?" All my muscles hurt, and I felt as though I had run a marathon.

"Jane is tired," Eleanor said.

"I just want to go to sleep."

Matilda frowned. "All right then, we will have a quick discussion about the case. I'll make some coffee."

"But Jane won't be able to sleep if she has any coffee," Eleanor protested.

"Nothing will be able to stop me from sleeping, trust me," I said. In fact, I thought coffee was a good idea because I didn't think I'd be able to get another word out without any.

I sat on the couch, dozing off, until Matilda handed me a mug of coffee. I wasted no time sipping some. After about five or so mouthfuls, I was more alert.

"I made it triple strength for you," Matilda said, sounding quite pleased with herself.

Well, that explained why it tasted so dreadful.

"Mr. Crumbles is annoyed with us for being out so late," Eleanor announced. "He is ignoring me."

Matilda, in turn, ignored Eleanor. "There were no surveillance devices in Dr. Ramsgate's office," Matilda informed me. "That means he can't be the Raven."

I gulped another mouthful of coffee. "I don't follow your line of reasoning."

Eleanor hurried to explain. "If he *was* the Raven, then he would have had all sorts of surveillance devices, video and audio, in his office."

Matilda waved her finger at Eleanor. "It doesn't mean he isn't the Raven, though. We must never assume anything."

For once, Eleanor agreed with her. "Quite so, quite so. But Jane, it's highly unlikely that Dr. Ramsgate is the Raven. If he *was* the Raven, then he would have plenty of surveillance devices in his office."

"You already said that," Matilda snapped.

"Yes, but Jane doesn't look as though she's listening. She keeps falling asleep."

I sat bolt upright. "I do not!" I took another sip of coffee for good measure.

Matilda tapped her chin and looked thoughtful. "I did think it was suspicious how Dr. Ramsgate left that file out on his desk for you to see and then went to make tea. I thought it was a trap, but maybe it was innocent, after all." She looked off into the distance before adding, "And at the risk of repeating what Eleanor has already repeated a million times, the Raven would most certainly have had surveillance devices in his office."

"Is it possible the Raven has the most up-to-date surveillance devices that your equipment couldn't detect?" I asked her.

"No, that's not possible," Eleanor told me. "However, the Raven would expect us to search the office, so that would explain the absence of devices." She went on to explain the intricacies of surveillance devices and how to detect them in minute detail.

I must have fallen asleep, because I awoke to hear Matilda say, "No wonder she fell asleep, Eleanor. You were boring her dreadfully."

"I wasn't bored," I said. "I *am* horribly tired. Where's my coffee?"

"I grabbed your cup in a remarkable display of quick reflexes the moment you fell asleep," Matilda told me. "Otherwise, you'd be wearing that coffee right now."

She handed me my cup, and I drained the rest in one go. It was only lukewarm, and I wondered how long I had been asleep. "So, where does that leave us now?" I asked them. "As far as suspects go, that is."

"Apart from Silas Greeves, we don't know any other elderly men," Matilda said. "Every elderly man connected with this case has to be treated as a suspect. We'll go through the guest list and the volunteer list and make a list of all men over eighty."

"But not tonight!" I said in alarm. "I have to get some sleep."

The sisters hurried to reassure me. Matilda

made a shooing motion with her right hand. "Yes, you go to sleep now, Jane. I'll have to get some sleep, as will Eleanor. Oh, that reminds me, the medical doctor."

"Dr. Smythe?" I asked her.

They both nodded. "I still think she could be the murderer," Matilda said, "and if she is, then her accomplice would be the Raven."

"Then we need to question Dr. Smythe," I said. "After we have had plenty of sleep," I added for good measure.

CHAPTER 11

I awoke just before dawn and then closed my eyes tightly, trying to will myself back to sleep. That was a habit from being raised Amish, getting up just before dawn.

After five minutes of trying to get back to sleep, I gave up and went down to the kitchen to make coffee. Mr. Crumbles sprinted down the stairs after me, meowing. I fed him before seeing to the coffee.

Matilda and Eleanor soon joined me. "Did you sleep well?" Matilda asked me.

"Yes, in the very short time that I had to sleep," I told her.

"I thought it all through in the night," she said. "You're going to go alone to speak with Dr. Smythe and Silas Greeves. But don't worry, I'm going to put a wire on you, and I'll be sitting outside in the car ready to save you if it all goes belly up."

"What about me?" Eleanor said.

"You'll have to replace Jane in Rebecca's shop, of course."

Eleanor looked as though she was about to complain but obviously thought the better of it. She shot me a weak smile.

Matilda pushed on. "Of course, both of us would like to go with you, but if they are connected with the Raven, then they'll expect people over the age of eighty."

"And I assume I'm to give them the standard line," I said. "I'm to tell them the police suspect me, and so I want to ask them if they noticed anything amiss."

Matilda nodded. "Precisely. And if Dr. Smythe isn't an accomplice of the Raven, then she might have noticed something."

"And if she *is* an accomplice of the Raven?" I stopped to pour coffee and looked at Matilda.

"Then she still might give something away. After all, she's a medical doctor, not a spy."

"Something occurred to me when I was trying to get back to sleep this morning," I told them.

Matilda was busy making herself coffee soup, dropping pieces of stale bread into a bowl of coffee. It was an Amish dish I had never gotten used to. "Well, get on with it, Jane," she said.

"If Dr. Smythe was the one who murdered Scarface, then why did she draw attention to the needle mark in his neck? Shouldn't she have pretended she thought it was a heart attack?"

Matilda shook her head. "No, that was a clever move on her part. She knew that drawing attention to that needle mark would throw suspicion off herself."

"I see. Well then, what if she refuses to see me today? She might be too busy with patients."

"Go to her clinic early and tell the receptionist that you're there on a personal matter. I'm sure Dr. Smythe will speak with you, even if she has to fit you in later in the morning between patients."

"I wish I had your confidence," I said.

"We've done this a million times." Eleanor's tone was nonchalant. "We wouldn't ask you to do this, Jane, but the matter is getting more urgent by the minute."

"What do you mean?" I asked, alarmed.

"Eleanor means that the Raven is on the lookout for us. Scarface obviously got wind of the fact that the Raven wanted to take both of us out, and so he came here to warn us. He covered his tracks well, of course, which is why the Raven hasn't found us. Still, the Raven is a determined and deadly person, and he'll be doing everything he can to track us down."

I yawned widely. "Okay, I'll speak with Dr. Smythe this morning."

"And we will use the new wire we acquired recently on you," Eleanor said. "It's the very latest technology."

Matilda looked up from slurping her coffee soup. "Are you certain, Eleanor? Shouldn't we use one of the older ones that we know works for sure? This is no time for experimentation."

Eleanor appeared quite put out. "No! What's the point of spending all that money on it if we're not going to use it? It's supposed to be the best thing ever!"

Mr. Crumbles fluffed up his tail and ran out of the room at her tone. Eleanor jumped up and hurried after him. "You scared Mr. Crumbles," she yelled at Matilda over her shoulder.

Matilda simply rolled her eyes and made herself some more coffee soup.

A few hours later, I was sitting in the car with

Matilda, and I was wearing a wire. "Are you sure it won't fall off me or something?" I asked.

"Eleanor and I are professionals, remember," Matilda said sternly. "It will work perfectly fine. Just remember to speak normally, and don't yell or anything. It will pick everything up."

The wire was attached to the small of my back. While it wasn't exactly uncomfortable, I was certainly aware of its presence.

The doctor's clinic was in a small, white building. It didn't look as though it was a large clinic. I took a deep breath and got out of the car. "Good luck," Matilda called after me.

I looked at my watch. It was just before eight-thirty. The front door was closed, but it opened when I pushed it gently.

The receptionist looked up from her desk. "Good morning," she said with a tight-lipped smile.

I walked over to her. "I'm Jane Delight," I began, but she interrupted me.

"What time is your appointment?"

I shook my head. "I don't have an appointment. I'm here on a personal matter, to speak with Dr. Smythe."

"Is she expecting you?"

"No, but…"

Once again, she interrupted me. "I'm afraid you'll have to make an appointment."

"But I'm not sick," I protested. I was about to say something else when Dr. Smythe walked into the room. "Alice, do you have the files for Mrs. Fitzgibbons?" She stopped in her tracks when she saw me. "Oh. Hello."

"Dr. Smythe, would you have a minute?" I asked. "It's about what happened the other night."

She turned back to the receptionist. "What time is my first appointment?"

The receptionist tapped away at her keyboard. "Nine."

Dr. Smythe beckoned to me. "Sure, come to my office."

I followed her into a pristine room. Everything was white—the tiles on the floor, the walls, the filing cabinets, the plantation shutters, even the computers were white. Numerous works of art hung on the walls. I idly wondered if she had claimed them as an office tax deduction.

"Please, take a seat." Dr. Smythe indicated I should sit on a deeply upholstered white chair.

I did so. "Dr. Smythe," I began, but she held up one hand, palm outward.

CONFECTIONS OF A PARTYGOER

"Please, call me Sue."

"Sue," I said. "My name is Jane Delight. I don't think we exchanged names the other night. Anyway, I'll come straight to the point."

She raised one eyebrow.

"Because I was the one who found the body, I suppose you could say, the police suspect me. They've been questioning me non-stop. I can't afford a good lawyer, and I'm afraid I'll go to prison for something I didn't do."

"Why would the police suspect you?" she asked.

"I can only assume they thought I was the one who jabbed him with the needle," I said. "I had never met the man, but I can't prove that. I'm worried the police are looking for somebody to take the fall. That's why I've decided I have to do some sleuthing."

She leaned forward and drummed her fingers on the table. "Sleuthing? That sounds dangerous. Surely, that could get you killed."

I wondered if she was threatening me. I took a deep breath and pushed on. "But what choice do I have?"

Just then, I heard a strange, gurgling sound. I looked around the room to see if she had a goldfish bowl, thinking it was something to do with a faulty filter, but there was none. The sound came again and was quite loud.

I realized, to my alarm, it was coming from the wire.

I raised my voice in an attempt to conceal the gurgling sounds. "And that's why I wanted to ask you if you happened to notice anyone with the victim before he died?"

She shook her head. "The police asked me that, but no, I didn't see anybody. I myself hadn't noticed the man until you called out to ask if there was a doctor in the room."

"Yes, I remember you had to move through the crowd to get to him. Did you notice anybody leaving the victim's direction?"

She appeared puzzled by my question. "Leaving the victim's direction?" she repeated.

"Did you notice anybody leaving the room at the time? That is to say, if somebody had injected the poor man, then that person would be in a hurry to leave the room."

She nodded slowly. "Oh yes, I see what you mean. No, all my attention was on the sick person. I assumed at first he was a victim of a heart attack."

The wired gurgled again.

"Do you have this problem often?" she asked me. "Have you eaten something you shouldn't?"

I was entirely confused. "What do you mean?"

"There's no need to be embarrassed, Jane. I'm a doctor. I'm referring to your serious flatulence problem."

Right on cue, the wire made an even more dreadful sound. My hand flew to my mouth. "Oh, it's not, um," I began, but words failed me. My cheeks flushed hot.

"Charcoal tablets can sometimes be of use in such cases," she continued. "Although, elevated gut sounds can occur if one hasn't eaten for a long time. Did you have breakfast?"

"Not enough," I said. I wanted to draw the attention back to my investigation, but the loud sounds coming from the wire were a distraction, to say the least. "Did you see a person in black walking away from the general direction of the victim?"

Dr. Smythe frowned and then said, "Yes, I do believe I did. Still, the people dressed in black were everywhere."

"You go to these events all the time, don't you? Dr. Ramsgate told me you're a regular patron."

She smiled broadly. "Yes, I am."

"Did you notice anything suspicious that night? Or anything out of the ordinary? Even something you might think was insignificant? It's really important."

She appeared to be giving the matter some thought. "No, it seemed like any other night. I didn't really notice anything out of the ordinary, nothing whatsoever."

Well, this was a dead end. "Some of the volunteers were dressed in black, weren't they?" She nodded. I added, "Did you notice anybody dressed in black who wasn't a volunteer?"

She shrugged. "I didn't look all that closely, to be honest."

I had hoped to get more out of this question session, but I had to admit defeat. "Oh well, thank you for your time."

"I'm afraid I haven't been of any help," she said.

"I appreciate your time, anyway." I stood up, but as I did so, my ankle turned and I tripped, landing heavily on her desk. I knocked over a photo. "I'm terribly sorry," I said.

"No harm done. It isn't broken."

I looked at the photo. "That's a lovely photo. Is that you with your father?"

"Yes." She took the photo from me and put it back on the desk.

Still, I had gotten a good look at the man. He was slightly taller than Dr. Smythe, which meant he was about the height of the Raven. He was clean-shaven, so I wondered if I would recognize him with a beard. What's more, he appeared to be in his eighties. That, in itself, was not suspicious, but it did give me pause. What if Dr. Smythe was the Raven's daughter?

I turned to go, but she called me back. "Jane, I don't want to embarrass you, but that's the most serious case of flatulence I've ever encountered. If you want to make an appointment to see me in a professional capacity, speak with my receptionist on your way out. I would urge you to do so. We can run some tests."

"Um, thank you," I said. My remarks were punctuated by a terrible, ongoing sound from the wire.

I walked as fast as I could to the car, my cheeks burning. I was certainly going to give Matilda and Eleanor a piece of my mind!

CHAPTER 12

I waited for Matilda to stop laughing. "It wasn't funny," I protested again. "I was embarrassed."

Matilda's response was to double over and clutch at her stomach harder.

I failed to see the funny side of it. "What if the wire had made different sounds and revealed I was wearing a wire, and what if Dr. Smythe is the Raven's daughter?" I said tersely. "Then she would have known I was associated with you two, her father's mortal enemies."

Matilda finally stopped laughing. "You have to have a sense of humor in this business."

"But I'm not in *your* business," I said through

clenched teeth. "That was really scary, not to mention embarrassing."

"So, you mentioned a photograph?"

I nodded. "It was turned away where only she could see it. If I hadn't knocked it over, I wouldn't have seen it at all."

"And you didn't recognize the man?"

I shrugged. "He was clean-shaven. If he had a beard now, I wouldn't recognize him. And I don't know how long ago that photo was taken, only he did look around the age of eighty or so."

"Isn't Dr. Smythe too young to have a father that age?" Matilda asked me.

"Oh! I hadn't thought of that. Are you thinking she could be a colleague of the Raven's?" I thought about it and then added, "But would a spy keep a photograph of a fellow spy on a desk?"

Matilda shrugged. "It does seem strange, but it's never safe to assume anything. So, how old would you estimate this Dr. Smythe to be?"

"She seems to be in her late twenties," I guessed. "If that man is her father, then she would have been born when he was around the age of fifty. That does seem perfectly reasonable to me."

Matilda's face fell. "Yes, it does. So maybe the man in the photo was actually her father, and we don't know whether he was the Raven or not. Just because somebody has a father who is fifty years older isn't at all suspicious. What *is* suspicious is that Dr. Smythe is the most likely person to have given Scarface the needle."

"So, what do we do now?" I asked her. "Will I drive back to Rebecca's cake store?"

Matilda shook her head vigorously. "No, we have to question Silas Greeves."

"By we, I hope you actually mean *we*," I said in the firmest tone I could muster. "Matilda, I flatly refuse to go in there wearing this wire."

Matilda opened her mouth to speak, but I held my hand in front of me, palm outward. "Nothing you can say will make me go in there wearing this wire. And I wouldn't feel comfortable going by myself without surveillance backup. No, Matilda, you'll have to come with me to question Silas Greeves."

Matilda appeared most put out. She tapped her chin again and again. After a long interval, she said, "Then I suppose that will be all right."

"I can tell him you're my aunt," I suggested.

Matilda shook her head vigorously. "Oh no, because if Silas Greeves is the Raven and discovers that I'm not your aunt, that will not be good, not good at all. No, in these circumstances it is best to stick as closely to the truth as possible."

"Then I'll tell him you're my housemate."

Matilda continued to shake her head. "No, don't tell him anything unless he asks. If he does ask, then tell him you're my housemate, but don't offer any personal information at all."

"Okay." I certainly had a lot to learn about the spying business. "Where does Silas Greeves live?"

Matilda gave me an address and added, "I'll direct you."

I wished Eleanor had been there in Matilda's place. Eleanor was a superb navigator, whereas Matilda's navigation skills weren't much better than her driving. Actually, Matilda was a superb driver when being pursued. The problem was that she always drove as though she was being pursued.

After going the wrong way about five times, I finally found Silas Greeves's apartment building. It was brick and looked like any other apartment building in the district.

The front door was in black glossy paint. We walked inside, under the bright blue awning, and discovered his apartment was on the second floor. I made for the elevator, but Matilda tapped my arm. "Let's take the stairs," she said.

I followed her up the stairs. Once again, I reminded myself that I needed to schedule some regular exercise.

Matilda knocked on the door. There was no response. I was about to ask what we should do next when she knocked again, more loudly this time. After a short interval, I heard footsteps making their way toward the door.

The door opened to reveal an elderly man. He was around the same height as Dr. Ramsgate, and he too had a thick white beard. "Who are you?" he said abruptly.

"I am Matilda, and this is Jane Delight."

He peered at Matilda and then at me. "I'm not buying anything!" He made to shut the door, but Matilda put her foot in it.

"We were at the art gallery party when Marvin Maze was murdered."

He let go of the door at once, as though it were electrified. He stared at us, not saying a word.

"I was the one who ran to his assistance," I said. "I'd like to ask some questions, if I may."

"Come in," he grunted. He stepped back, and we walked inside. He led us through a small kitchen. It seemed cluttered, rather than outrightly messy. Every surface was covered with some sort of kitchen utensil, and one of the cupboards didn't have doors, leaving its contents on display. The kitchen cupboards above the countertop likewise held items stacked high.

Once through the kitchen, which was comprised of one wall, he led us to a gray couch on which were perched several lime green cushions.

"Please sit," he said. He skirted the wooden coffee table on which was a fake potted plant and fetched a chair from the old wooden kitchen table. He dragged the chair across the polished floor with a series of squeaks, placed it in front of us, and proceeded to sit upon it.

"I remember you," he said. "You asked if there was a doctor in the room."

I nodded. "That's right."

"Why did you call out for a doctor? Didn't Marvin look well?"

"Not well at all," I said.

"It was good of you to act so quickly even though it didn't help in the end."

I didn't know what to say, so I simply nodded. Then I remembered why I was there. "The police suspect me," I told him.

His surprise seemed genuine. "Why would they suspect you? Did you know Marvin?"

I shook my head. "No, I saw him for the first time only seconds before I had to call out for help. I assume the police suspect me because they don't have any other suspects."

"That doesn't seem fair," he said.

"It isn't fair," I added. "I'm going to have to do some sleuthing in order to clear my name."

He frowned hard. "I don't know if I can be of any help. I'd like to help though," he added as an apparent afterthought.

"Did Marvin have any friends?" I asked him.

He shrugged. "He kept to himself. He was nice enough. He just kept to himself," he said again.

"So, you didn't know him well?"

He jutted out his bottom lip and shook his head slowly. "Not really. I mean, we chatted a lot, being around the same age and everything. He was in much better shape than I am, though."

Matilda was sitting close to me, and she gave me a slight jab in the ribs.

"Do you have health issues?" I hoped that was what I was supposed to ask. The jabbing in my ribs had stopped, so I took that as an answer.

"I've had a bad back for some time, and it's

been getting worse lately," he told me. "Dr. Ramsgate didn't want me to be one of the figures in black at the party."

"Why not?" Matilda asked him.

"He didn't want me to go at all! It was because of those art installations. You know, they can be dangerous."

I agreed. "That's for sure." I thought of Damon's ankle. "But you did go to the party. Were you one of the men in black?"

His face lit up. "Yes, Dr. Ramsgate let me after I complained a lot. I don't know how many warnings he gave me about keeping away from the art installations though. Still, I know he was only thinking of my welfare."

"Did you see anybody dressed as one of the black figures who wasn't supposed to be, that is, somebody who wasn't a volunteer?"

"No, I don't think I did," he said pensively, stroking his beard.

"Can you be sure?"

He shook his head. "I can't remember. I don't think I was surprised to see anyone else who was dressed in black." He shrugged. "Maybe I'm just mixed up. The night was a terrible shock, you see."

"Yes, of course it was," I said in soothing tones.

"And it wouldn't have helped that the hoods were quite big and would easily have hidden the wearers' faces." He nodded. I pushed on. "Where were you when Marvin died?"

"I wasn't too far from him, as a matter of fact," he said. He pulled a handkerchief from his pocket and dabbed at his eyes.

I remembered seeing him at the time dabbing at his eyes in the very same manner. "Did you see anybody hurrying away from Marvin just before he died?"

He took the handkerchief away from his eyes. "Yes, one of the figures in black. He headed for the restrooms. He seemed to be in a hurry. I thought maybe he had eaten something he shouldn't."

"I don't suppose you got a look at his face?"

He shook his head. "No, I didn't see his face."

My spirits fell. "How long have you worked at the art gallery?"

"I don't work there. I'm a volunteer."

"How long have you volunteered at the Art Gallery?" Matilda asked him.

"Possibly fifteen years?" He said it as a question and scratched his head. "And are you this lady's mother?"

Matilda chuckled. "No, we work together. We were both helping with the catering."

"Do the police suspect you too?"

"I don't believe so," Matilda said. "However, they do suspect Jane, and as much as I don't approve of her taking matters into her own hands, I agreed to help her try to solve the case." Matilda shot me a stern look. "I keep telling her she should leave it to the police, but she won't listen to me."

"I'm sure the police will solve it," Silas snapped.

Matilda elbowed me in the ribs again. I thought of another question I should ask him. "So, were you volunteering at the art gallery before Dr. Ramsgate took over as director?"

He nodded. "Yes, it was Henry, um, somebody before him." He tapped his head. "Oh dear, I've forgotten his surname. What was it? Oh dear, I can't remember. Anyway, we called him Henry, by his first name. Dr. Ramsgate is oh so pretentious. He certainly wouldn't allow anybody to call him by his first name." His tone dripped with disapproval.

"Does Dr. Ramsgate have any friends?" I asked him.

He seemed to think my question funny. After

he recovered laughing, he said, "No. Nobody likes him. He's a real loner, that one."

"But surely, he has at least one friend?" I prompted him.

"He did have a secretary, but she retired a few years ago, and he didn't replace her."

"What was her name?" Matilda asked him.

"Cindy Bellamy. She wasn't very nice, either. Two peas in a pod, they were. I wasn't surprised when he didn't replace her, though. Why pay someone when you can get the volunteers to do the work?" His face formed a mask of displeasure. "Now, is that all you want to ask me? I don't mean to be rude, but I need to take a nap." He stood, and we stood too.

"Thanks for your help," I said. "If you think of anything else, could you call me?"

"Yes, I will, but I'm sure I won't think of anything else."

I opened my purse and pulled out a piece of paper and a pen. I wrote my name and phone number on the paper and handed it to him. "Just in case," I said.

He smiled and showed us to the door. I noticed he was walking stiffly, more stiffly after he had been sitting for a while.

Once we were outside and out of earshot, I made to say something, but Matilda shook her head. We were almost at the entrance when an elderly woman called to us. We walked back to her apartment door. "Were you visiting old Silas Greeves?"

She looked at least as old as Silas was, maybe even older, so I was surprised that she had described him as old. I admitted that we had been to see him.

"You're the first visitors he's ever had," she said. "I've never known him to have visitors before. Are you relatives?"

"Friends of friends," Matilda told her. "How long has he lived in this apartment building? Fifteen years?"

"Only about four or five years," she told us. She tapped one finger on the side of her head. "The elevator doesn't go all the way to the roof, if you get my meaning. If he told you he's lived here for fifteen years, he's wrong. It wouldn't have been more than four or five."

Something occurred to me. "He said he'd been volunteering at the art gallery for fifteen years."

She seemed to think that was awfully funny. "Oh no, I know he only started volunteering there after he moved here, and like, I said that was only four or five years ago."

"How do you know that?" Matilda said, her tone overly friendly. "Did he tell you?"

The woman shook her head. "No, a friend of mine did. She was the secretary there, but she retired recently."

"Cindy Bellamy?" I asked.

The woman looked surprised. "Do you know her?"

"No, but Silas mentioned her."

Matilda took over the conversation. "Can you keep a secret?"

That woman rubbed her hands together. "Oh yes, I certainly can. What secrets do you have to tell me?"

"We're private investigators," Matilda said. "But you can't tell a soul."

The woman shook her head vigorously. "No, I certainly won't. You can trust me."

"We are investigating the murder of Marvin Maze. He was murdered at the art gallery the other night. That's why we were questioning Silas."

Her mouth fell open. "You don't think he did it?"

Matilda hurried to reassure her. "No, we don't, but he has helped us with our inquiries. We would also like to question Cindy Bellamy. Would you have her contact details?"

The woman looked around the empty corridor. "Wait right there, won't you?" She popped back into her apartment, shutting the door behind her. Only moments later, she returned and thrust a piece of paper into Matilda's hands. "You can tell her I gave this to you. My name is Violet Peavesbody. And your secret is safe with me." She winked.

CHAPTER 13

As soon as we were back in my car, I turned to Matilda. "Do you think Silas is the Raven?"

She shrugged. "I'm keeping an open mind. Any man over eighty who was at the party is a suspect."

I agreed. "And he lied—or at least was mistaken—about the length of time he'd been volunteering at the art gallery, as well as the length of time he'd been living in his apartment."

"The time certainly fits with the time the Raven escaped."

I felt a little nauseous. "Do you think he was suspicious of you? He did ask if you were my mother."

Matilda grimaced. "That was a cause for concern, as was him getting the timeline wrong, but there could be an innocent explanation. We will discuss it with Eleanor later, but for now, you and I have to go to Scarface's house."

"What, now?" I was about to protest, but Matilda spoke first.

"And we will wear the old man disguises again. If the Raven does have eyes on us, he will think you're Eleanor. Your build is completely different from Eleanor's, and so that will help throw him off the track."

"Look, I'm no spy," I began, "but it's extremely obvious, even to me, that the Raven will expect you and Eleanor to go to Scarface's house. What if he has rigged something to explode when somebody enters the place?"

Matilda chuckled. "You've been watching too much TV."

I crossed my arms over my chest. "You can't tell me it doesn't happen."

Matilda sobered at once. "You're right, it does happen. And I'm certain the Raven has already searched Marvin's house by now. Still, we need to search it."

"But what's the point?" I asked her. "You

yourself said the Raven would have already searched it. What can possibly be left for us to find?"

"Leave the spying to me, Jane," Matilda said with a wink. "The Raven didn't know Scarface like I did. Let's drive somewhere remote, change into the men's clothes again, and then dump your car."

"Dump my car?" I shrieked in alarm.

Matilda chuckled again. "That's just a figure of speech, Jane. We'll need to leave your car somewhere, walk a considerable distance disguised as old men, take a taxi to within a few blocks of a car hire place, and hire a car. I have the route all mapped out to avoid cameras."

It dawned on me for the first time. "Can the Raven hack cameras on the street?"

"We should never leave anything to chance," Matilda simply said.

And so, I found myself driving to Amish country, to a quiet road where I would be able to see cars or buggies coming in the distance. "I'm not using glue on your wig this time," Matilda said, "since we won't be doing any gymnastic activities. I'll use wig grip instead."

We changed into the old man disguises, and then Matilda instructed me to drive to town. I had blisters from the shoes of the previous night, but Matilda had provided a pair of thicker socks this time.

"If the Raven does see us, either in person or see footage of us, there's a chance he'll think Eleanor and I were men all the time," Matilda said cheerily. "That will be a big help, if he doesn't intend to do away with us at Scarface's house."

A feeling of dread settled over me. "Is Scarface's house in a remote area?" I asked her.

"Yes, of course."

"But isn't that unsafe? I mean, won't that be easier for the Raven to attack us?"

"Oh, don't trouble yourself, Jane. We're in danger from the Raven anywhere, remote house or otherwise." She smiled and nodded as she spoke.

"That's hardly reassuring," I told her.

Matilda instructed me to park in an undercover parking area. "I saw a camera as we came in," I said.

"We didn't need to avoid *that* one," Matilda told me. "We only need to avoid the significant ones in certain places. All right, now we have to walk to get a taxi."

As soon as she got out of the car, she acted like an elderly man.

It seemed to take us an age to get to where Matilda wanted to get a taxi. We were walking slowly and were stooped over. I did my best not to look around because Matilda had told me that would be suspicious.

Finally, we were in a hire car and I was driving to the location we had been given as Scarface's house.

"I hadn't realized I would have to give fake ID at the car hire," I said to Matilda as we drove away.

"What?" She swiveled around to stare at me. "Did you think you could give your real ID while dressed as an old man?"

"I hadn't really thought about it," I admitted. "Where did you get the fake ID from?"

Matilda shrugged. "Eleanor and I keep fake IDs on hand, of course. You never know when they'll come in handy."

I took one hand off the steering wheel to rub my forehead. This was all so crazy, and what if the Raven was waiting for us? When I said this aloud to Matilda, she didn't seem worried.

"The Raven can't sit outside Scarface's house night and day just waiting for us to show up, and if anything, he would be more likely to show up at night. No, he'd have surveillance equipment on the place. At least, that's what I would do. Stakeouts are so dreadfully boring, and nobody has time for that sort of thing."

I hoped she was right. "And what if he does have a bomb set to go off as soon as we open a window or a door?" I asked her.

"That's hardly likely, because he would know the police would go to the victim's house in a case of homicide," Matilda said.

Undaunted, I pushed on. "But what if he waits until after the police go to the house? The police would have already been to the house by now. What if he set up bombs after the police went to the house?"

"The police sometimes go to a homicide victim's house more than once," Matilda said. "And, of course, the Raven would know that only too well. No, I'm fairly confident the Raven has surveillance equipment around."

"But you can't be sure?"

"It never pays to be sure about anything, not in my line of work," Matilda said. "But I do have equipment that will help."

To my relief, Scarface's house wasn't as remote as I thought. It was less than half a mile from the nearest house. And while that wouldn't have helped if the Raven was there to kill us, seeing another house nearby did offer me a small measure of relief.

Matilda told me to park in the driveway. "Shouldn't we be sneaking around the back or something?" I asked her.

"No, we are going to act as though we have every right to be here," she said. "Jane, just follow my lead. I'm going to go in first, and then I'll come out and wave to you. And remember not to speak, no matter what."

"Be careful," I admonished her.

Matilda walked to the front door and knocked. The next thing I knew, she was in the house. She must have picked that lock very cleverly, because I was watching her the whole time and didn't notice. I expected her baggy suit had hidden her actions.

It seemed like an age before Matilda returned to the door and waved, but at least the house didn't explode. I got out of the car when she waved and walked slowly over to the door. As soon as I was inside, Matilda said to me, "Frank, there were surveillance cameras inside, but I hope I've disabled them all." She shot me a stern look.

I nodded, following her instructions that I wasn't to speak at all.

Matilda kept speaking. "You are not to touch anything. If you see anything, come over and let me know."

I nodded. Matilda was doing an awfully good job of speaking in a man's voice. An actor could not have done better.

I looked around the living room. I had no idea what I was supposed to be looking for, and I thought it pointless that I was there, given that I was totally untrained as a spy.

The house was sparsely furnished and, in fact, appeared to be wholly furnished from a thrift store. A tattered old, green couch was the only seating in the room, and the old wooden coffee table in front of it had seen better days. The television against the far wall did, however, look new and expensive.

I walked over to the kitchen when Matilda was looking in the fridge. I looked over her shoulder. Nothing appeared to be suspicious. I watched as Matilda took each item out one by one. She took a tub of ice cream from the freezer, took off the lid, and looked inside it, before putting it back in.

To me, it seemed a consummate waste of time and a dangerous waste of time at that. I was half expecting the Raven to turn up at any minute, guns blazing.

Matilda beckoned me into a bedroom which opened off the tiny kitchen. There was only one bed in it, as well as a closet. I stood there while Matilda searched every item in the closet.

There were two bedrooms in the house, and the other bedroom was completely empty. Matilda poked the carpet as if expecting to find hidden panels under it.

When she had finished her search, she tapped my arm and pointed to the front door. I nodded and followed her. "You go and get in the car," she said. "I'll lock up."

When we were safely in the car, I took a deep breath and let it out slowly. "You didn't find anything," I said as I drove away.

"Of course not," Matilda said. "I knew I wouldn't find anything."

I was confused. "Then why did we go there?"

"We went there so the Raven would see us and hopefully think that Eleanor and I had really been men all along," Matilda told me. "That's why I specifically told you to stay in character the whole time."

My temples throbbed, and I knew I was going

to get a terrible headache. "So, I was just there as a decoy?"

"No, not a decoy, exactly," she said. "Eleanor and I will be much safer if the Raven thinks we were really men the whole time. Hopefully, he thinks we were men pretending to be women back in the day. If he's looking for men now, then we will be much safer."

One thing puzzled me. "But didn't you say you had disabled all the surveillance devices?"

"Yes, I did, the ones inside the house, that is. The Raven would have placed other devices outside the house."

I gasped. "Do you mean I was caught on camera?"

"Of course!" Matilda's tone was triumphant. "That was the whole point of the exercise, to trick the Raven into thinking Eleanor and I were men."

I looked in the rear vision mirror. "There's a black car following us."

"That can't be good." Matilda swiveled around to look. "Take a left here."

I did so. "Still following us," I told her.

"Take the next right."

I took the next right, and so did the car following us.

"I'll have to drive," Matilda said. "Thankfully, we hired this V-8 turbo-diesel off-road vehicle."

I made to slow down, but Matilda shrieked, "What are you doing?"

"I thought you wanted me to pull over so you could drive?" I asked her. "And that car is getting closer."

"We'll have to swap places while the car is going at full speed," Matilda told me. "What a shame we haven't practiced this before. Oh well, never mind."

"*Never mind?*" I shrieked. "Are you mad? We can't swap places unless I stop the car first!"

"Of course, we can. I've done it many a time." Matilda's tone was soothing. "Jane, let me take the wheel, and you climb into the back seat. Once you're in there, keep your head down."

I was about to protest, but I could see Matilda was determined. I had no choice but to do as she said.

I let go of the steering wheel. Matilda's left hand was already on it. I squeezed past her and flung myself in a heap onto the back seat before falling to the floor.

The car swung violently. For a horrible moment, I thought we had run off the road at speed, but then the car accelerated, and I knew Matilda was firmly in control of the vehicle.

"Are you okay?" I called out.

"Yes, keep your head down," Matilda said. "Get on the floor. It's definitely the Raven, and he's going to try to run us off the road. I wonder if Silas Greeves is the Raven, and he followed us." Her tone was calm. She might as well have been discussing the weather.

I could hear gunshots whizzing past the car. "He's shooting at us!" I squealed.

"No, he's only shooting at the tires," Matilda said. "This is personal. He doesn't want to shoot us, not from a distance at any rate. Oh dear, I hope he doesn't shoot the car. How will we explain that?"

With those less than reassuring words, the car swung violently this way and that. I assumed Matilda was taking evasive action, making it harder for the Raven to shoot out the tires. Either that, or she was just a very bad driver.

I shut my eyes as the car went faster and faster, all the while flinging me forcefully this way and that.

After what seemed an age, Matilda said, "Hang on, I'm going through some fields."

I heard a crash and looked up to see bits of what looked like timber flying past the windows. "Did you hit something?" I called to her.

"Only a gate," Matilda said in a matter-of-fact tone. "I didn't have time to stop and open it, obviously."

A good five minutes later, Matilda slowed down. "We've lost him," she said. "Hopefully, there's no damage to the car. The only thing we hit was that old, wooden gate."

"Weren't there two gates?" I asked her.

Matilda chuckled again. "You can sit up now, Jane. No, there was only one gate. I went out of that field the way we came in. The Raven's car is stuck in a creek."

"Are you sure?" I sat up and looked out of the window. There wasn't another car in sight.

"Yes, I'm certain. We will take this car through a car wash and then return it. We will have to be much more careful with our exit plan now, because the Raven got our plates. He'll trace the car to the car hire, and then he'll try to trace us from there. It's going to be a long time before we get home today, Jane."

"Great," I muttered.

CHAPTER 14

I was by myself in the cupcake store for a few hours the following morning as Rebecca was taking food to one of the elderly ladies in the community.

She greeted me with a smile as she walked in the door. "How was business today?"

"*Gut*," I said, lapsing into Pennsylvania Dutch. In English, I added, "We sold out of sugar cream pie cupcakes."

Rebecca smiled widely. "I will have to bake some more. And your morning was good?"

I nodded. "At least nobody shot at me."

Rebecca looked alarmed. "Shot at you? What do you mean?"

I collected my thoughts and gave myself a

mental slap. "Just a joke, a bad joke." I forced a smile. I didn't like lying to my twin sister, but Rebecca would be in danger if she knew what was really going on. No, she could never know that Matilda and Eleanor were retired international spies.

Rebecca went to the kitchen, presumably to start baking, when the door opened. I looked up, and to my surprise, Dr. Ramsgate walked in.

"Dr. Ramsgate!" I exclaimed.

He peered at me. "I'm terribly sorry, I have forgotten your name again. It's my age, you see." He offered his hand, and I shook it.

I doubted it was his age. He looked to be the same age as Matilda or Eleanor, and they were as sharp as tacks. Maybe he simply couldn't be bothered remembering my name. "It's Jane," I told him again. "Jane Delight."

"What a *delightful* name." He chuckled at his own joke.

I looked at him expectantly. Was he here to buy cupcakes? I had never seen him in the store before.

"You must be wondering why I'm here?"

I smiled and nodded.

"I want to help with your investigation." I noticed for the first time he was carrying a large, black leather briefcase. He reached inside for some papers and put them on the countertop in front of me. "The police came to see me early this morning and were asking me questions about you, your sister, and the other ladies who work here."

"They were?"

He nodded slowly. "If I might be honest, my dear, I thought you were exaggerating or maybe had a case of nerves when you told me the police suspected you."

He shot me an apologetic look before pushing on. "But after this morning, it's clear to me that the police *do* suspect you, either acting alone or with the people who work in this store."

"That's terrible," I said. I was about to say that the police hadn't questioned me again, but I realized I needed to keep that pretense going. "Yes, I knew they suspected me," I said as an afterthought. "It's very kind of you to want to help me clear my name."

He waved one hand in the air, looking for all the world like a conductor. "I'm afraid my intentions are not quite as altruistic as you might suppose. I cannot have the art gallery tainted with an unsolved murder. Why, I have had barely a soul cross the door since the other night." He shook his head in disgust. "Until this murder is solved, business will continue to be bad. And we do have another exhibition opening party planned for next month, but it won't possibly be able to go ahead if the murder has not been solved by then."

"I hadn't thought of that," I said. That, at least, was true.

Dr. Ramsgate was still speaking. "A terrible business, a terrible business indeed. I simply cannot understand how the murderer could commit such a heinous crime in front of over a hundred witnesses and get away with it. It's ridiculous, I tell you!" His face turned beet red, and he slapped the countertop hard.

I opened my mouth to say something, but Dr. Ramsgate continued to rant. "The police are incompetent, I tell you! Incompetent! It's obvious to anybody that the murderer was at the party." He tapped his index finger on the papers he had dropped on the countertop. "This is the guest list. I have looked through it to see if I could find anything suspicious, but I fear I am too close to the situation. Jane, would you and your friends be so kind as to discover whether you can find anybody suspicious in the guest list?"

"Of course," I said. "I'd be happy to. Anything that could clear my name."

Rebecca walked out of the back room and stared at Dr. Ramsgate. I was afraid she had forgotten who he was, so I said, "Rebecca, you would remember Dr. Ramsgate, the director from the art gallery."

Rebecca shot him a smile. "Of course. How are you today, Dr. Ramsgate?"

"Very well, thank you. I was telling Jane here that the police questioned me at length this morning about the two of you and the other two ladies who work in your shop."

"Oh, they don't work in my shop," Rebecca said. "They do help out from time to time though. Matilda and Eleanor are Jane's housemates."

I fervently wished Rebecca hadn't told him that, but too late, the information was out.

"I haven't had a chance to meet them," he said. "I only saw them from a distance. They seem quite charming ladies."

"Yes, they are," I said.

"Are they relatives of yours?"

Rebecca chuckled. "No, Matilda and Eleanor have never been Amish. Jane and I are twin sisters, you see."

Dr. Ramsgate nodded. "I do believe I knew that. And have you known the other ladies for a long time?"

I was at once suspicious. Why was he asking questions about Matilda and Eleanor? Could Dr. Ramsgate be the Raven, after all?

"Yes, they used to rent the apartment above the store from me," Rebecca told him.

"The taller one reminded me of my late wife," Dr. Ramsgate said wistfully. "I had quite a shock when I saw her. Is she married?"

"Her husband died some years ago," I lied.

Rebecca appeared shocked. "I didn't know Eleanor had been married?"

I plastered what I hoped was a sad look on my face. "She doesn't like to talk about it."

Rebecca appeared to be thinking it over. "I'll make sure I don't mention it to her."

"Maybe she's happy with the current man she is seeing," Dr. Ramsgate said, his tone nonchalant.

"She's not seeing anybody now," Rebecca said.

Dr. Ramsgate's face lit up.

I wished there was some way I could stop Rebecca and Dr. Ramsgate from talking. It's clear he wanted to know more about Matilda and Eleanor. Were his motives nefarious, or did he simply have a crush on Eleanor? I didn't have a clue, but the questions were making me nervous.

Thankfully, Dr. Ramsgate changed the subject. He reached into his briefcase and pulled out another folder, this one a much thinner file. "And here's a list of the volunteers who were present at the party. There are not many, you see, and I must tell you, I didn't know them all personally. We take whatever volunteers we can get, I'm afraid." He stroked his long white beard.

I thanked him. I looked at the list of names and made a show of being interested. Of course, I had already seen photos of the lists. "So, I have to look through these lists and do some research to see if anybody listed here had a grudge against the victim?"

"Yes, that would be good."

Rebecca tugged on my sleeve. "Jane, please tell me you're not investigating again."

Dr. Ramsgate raised one bushy white eyebrow. "Again?" he repeated.

Rebecca appeared somewhat embarrassed. "Jane likes to do some amateur sleuthing, as she calls it."

I was pleased that she said that. That would make me seem less suspicious to Dr. Ramsgate if he was, in fact, the Raven. Yet he had been working at the gallery for eight to ten years. When he had started working at the gallery, the Raven was already incarcerated. If indeed the Raven had murdered the real Dr. Ramsgate and assumed his identity, then surely somebody would have noticed. There would be people who had been clients of the art gallery for more than four or five years. I would have to track down those people.

Dr. Ramsgate spoke again and broke me from my reverie. "Jane, if I can be of any assistance in your amateur sleuthing, as you call it, please don't hesitate to call me." With a flourish, he produced a gold-embossed business card from his pocket and pressed it into my hands. "Too many years of hard work have gone into the art gallery to have it ruined by such an unpleasant event."

He smiled and turned away. He had only taken five or so steps when he returned. "I almost forgot." He handed me four envelopes. "These contain invitations to the Fundraiser Ball. I know it's short notice, but I want you to attend. The murderer is likely to attend as well. Feel free to give the invitations to any of your associates. If you notice anything untoward at the ball, please inform me at once."

With that, he took his leave.

I was left cold and shaken. Rebecca had told him too much about Matilda and Eleanor. If he *was* the Raven, then his only purpose coming here was to get information about the sisters. And now he knew they lived with me, and it would be no trouble for him to find my address. "I have to make a call," I said to Rebecca. I had to warn the sisters.

CHAPTER 15

I cut the engine and glanced at my reflection in the rear vision mirror. I looked gorgeous, and by gorgeous, I meant the bags under my eyes looked a little lighter than usual, and my hair had actually decided not to look like a hot mess that morning.

"I didn't bring Mr. Crumbles," Eleanor said proudly. She was sitting in the front passenger seat.

I nodded. "I know."

"I didn't bring Mr. Crumbles, despite the fact he's my attack cat, and despite the fact I bought him an attack cat outfit."

"There is," I replied, trying to sound measured, "no such thing as an official attack cat outfit."

"Then how did I buy Mr. Crumbles one?"

"Eleanor, you bought him a Batman costume."

"Batman attacks people."

"Mr. Crumbles hates his Batman costume so much he is currently lying face down on the carpet, refusing to move."

"That's because I was cross with him," Matilda said regretfully. She was sitting in the back seat. "He kept following me around, meowing, even though I fed him a million times."

Eleanor ignored Matilda and addressed me. "He just needs to get used to how fearsome he looks. He saw his reflection in the mirror and got a bit of a shock. Jane, I must tell you the training words for Mr. Crumbles."

"Training words?" I echoed.

"Yes. I've been training Mr. Crumbles to attack a mannequin. To put him on notice, you must say, 'Alert!' and to get him to attack, you say, 'Face Hugger!'"

"Face Hugger?" I repeated.

Eleanor appeared most put out. "Jane, this is important. For an attack cat to be managed correctly, you must use the correct training words."

I sighed. "Right. Okay. Well, we're off to collect Damon. No sneaking attack cats into the hospital, and no staring at the bottoms of deranged patients who have escaped."

"Frances didn't seem deranged to me," Matilda said thoughtfully.

"He stole my car," I reminded her, "while completely nude."

"Who hasn't?" Matilda replied.

"Wait, um," I sputtered. "What?" I certainly hoped she was joking.

The sisters did not seem alarmed that Dr. Ramsgate had asked questions about them, but maybe they were hiding their true feelings from me so as not to alarm me. They had both said that we had to carry on as usual, as that would seem less suspicious. They had told me that if Dr. Ramsgate was the Raven, that he would be looking into everybody over eighty who was at the party, and they reminded me that he didn't know that that they, as their spy selves, were sisters. It did reassure me, but only a little.

I stepped from the car and followed Matilda and Eleanor into the hospital. I was relieved to see Damon was looking much better. He was already packed and ready to go, and despite the fact he had crutches, the policy was we had to wheel him to the door.

"I'll wheel him," Matilda offered.

Damon, perhaps remembering how crazily she drove, and myself, remembering how she had just outrun the Raven in the hire car, both bellowed, "No!"

In the end, Damon let me wheel him to the car. He sat in the front passenger seat, while Matilda and Eleanor sat in the back, whining and pinching each other and asking to go to McDonald's.

We had not driven two blocks when I heard a knocking sound under the car. At least, that's where I thought it was coming from. I glanced over at Damon, but only momentarily, because I didn't want to run a red light.

"Am I going mad?" I asked.

"Yes," Matilda and Eleanor both said in unison.

"I hear it too," Damon said. He craned his neck over his shoulder. "Pull over."

He didn't need to ask me twice. I pulled over, and the four of us jumped from the car. Matilda, Eleanor, and I stood back from the car, while Damon used his crutches to move in on the trunk.

"If only we had an attack cat right about now," Eleanor said. She tapped her leg, right where I knew the pistol was hiding, and gave me a significant look.

I turned to Damon. "Damon, shouldn't we call the cops?"

"I *am* a cop."

"You're a detective. You turn up *after* the crime has been committed, not during."

"I've got this under control," Damon said. He puffed out his chest, which caused Matilda to giggle like a schoolgirl.

"My husband is so masculine."

"He's not your husband," I hissed.

"He is my husband when he is medicated," Matilda replied. "Or at least, so he thinks."

"Okay, stand back. I'm opening the trunk now." Damon opened the trunk and then jumped back with a shout.

Frances jumped out of the trunk. He was wearing a pink nightgown and pink, furry slippers. He bopped a surprised Damon on the nose, winked at Matilda, and then took off down the road.

"We've aided in the escape of a fugitive," Eleanor shrieked.

"He's not a fugitive," I replied. "He's just a silly old man."

Matilda smiled. "I'm going to invite him to join us for dinner."

"Matilda!" I cried. "You can't be serious."

Matilda was not listening. She pulled up her skirt and took off down the road after Frances. I didn't even know Matilda had that amount of speed in her legs.

"Somebody stop her," Damon said, but Eleanor and I merely sighed.

"Let her go," I said. "She can call if she needs a ride home after she catches up to Frances."

Still, I didn't actually think Matilda would catch Frances. Imagine my surprise, when she turned up at the house an hour later with Frances on her arm.

"Can Frances come for dinner?" Matilda asked sweetly.

"Sorry about the attire." France gestured to his nightgown. "I had to borrow them. The nurses took my clothes."

"No, Matilda," I said. "Frances needs to go back to the hospital. I'll get my keys and drive him myself."

"But we can take him back after dinner," Matilda protested. Frances pouted.

"Don't let that crazy person in here," Eleanor called out from the kitchen.

"But I'm your sister," Matilda replied.

"She means Frances," I said.

Eleanor walked out. "Come on, then. Come inside before I change my mind."

Rebecca and Ephraim were visiting people in the community that night, and I was going to drive Damon to their house after dinner. Billy had been locked up until our return.

When we were all sitting at the table, about to eat roast chicken, Frances suddenly spoke. "Get a psychic." The remark was addressed to Damon.

"Get a what?" Damon looked stunned.

"A psychic. I often used a psychic when I was on a case."

Damon looked doubtful. "Did they help solve any of the crimes?"

"No, not at all," Frances said with a laugh. "But I always knew which star sign I was compatible with, which is why I have been divorced five times."

"But, if you were so compatible, then why didn't your five marriages work?"

"Oh, I never listen to psychics." Frances

speared a piece of broccoli with his fork. "Complete nutters."

"What's a nutter?" I asked him.

"It's a British expression meaning somebody who is nuts. I've seen it on TV."

"Yes," Damon said. "Poor you, having to spend so much time with *complete nutters*."

Damon shot me a meaningful look. I almost kicked him under the table, but I remembered his broken ankle just in time.

"Do you have any idea who did it?" Frances addressed the remark to Damon.

Damon looked blank. "Did what?"

Frances gestured to his mouth to show he was chewing. After an interval, he swallowed loudly and said, "The murder at the art gallery, of course. You told me you were investigating it."

Damon appeared confused. "I did?"

Frances nodded vigorously. "Yes, when you were in the hospital."

"I don't remember. It must've been when I was reacting to the medication."

Frances pushed on. "You said you tripped over a painting at the art gallery when you went there to investigate a murder."

"That's right, but I didn't trip over a painting, it was a weird art installation."

Frances frowned. "A what?"

I hurried to explain. "An art installation. It's sort of like a sculpture, and they were supposed to be interactive, although there were big signs on them warning people not to touch them."

For some reason, this seemed to make sense to Frances. "Oh yes, that's so typical of artists." He nodded slowly as he spoke. "And Damon told me that you were there too, Jane?"

"Yes, I was. My sister, Rebecca, was catering the cupcakes."

"Rebecca and her husband, Ephraim, live only a short distance away," Damon told Frances. "You would have passed their house on your way here. I'm actually staying with them at the moment."

"So, why aren't you having dinner there?"

I spoke before Damon did. I was concerned for him. He looked tired, with dark circles under his eyes, and I could see he wasn't his usual self. No wonder, after what he had been through. "Rebecca and her husband are visiting other people in the community."

"What community?"

"The Amish community. They're Amish."

Frances pursed his lips. "Now I'm confused. Did you say Amish? But Jane, you're not Amish, are you? Or are you some sort of Very New Order Amish?"

I chuckled. "No, Rebecca is my twin sister, and I was raised Amish, but I left after my *rumspringa*."

"Your what?"

Matilda offered Frances some bread rolls. "You're not from around these parts, are you?"

"No," was his only response.

I explained. "Amish youth go on *rumspringa*. They stop living as Amish for a time and live as *Englischers*. Oh, that means non-Amish people."

"Not people from England?"

I shook my head. "No. Oh, I mean yes, you're right, not people from England. An *Englischer* is simply a non-Amish person. So, most *rumspringas* last about a year, and at the end of the year, the Amish youth is free to decide whether they return to the Amish or continue as an *Englischer*."

"I think I saw something like that in a movie," Frances said. "If they don't return to the Amish, are they shunned?"

I chuckled again. "Oh, goodness me, no! Of course not! Everyone is happy with whatever decision the youth makes. And besides, people don't get baptized until after their *rumspringa*, and only people who are baptized can be shunned."

Matilda wagged her finger at Frances. "You can't believe everything you see on TV," she said. "Would you like some applesauce?"

"The way to a man's heart is through his stomach," Eleanor said in little more than a whisper.

Matilda shot her a look.

"Did any of you know the victim?" Francis asked us.

I narrowed my eyes and looked at him. He certainly was asking lots of questions. What's more, he was over the age of eighty. I went cold all over. Could Frances possibly be the Raven? He wasn't at the party. But could I be sure he wasn't there? Could he have dressed as one of the people in black?

No, Silas had said he hadn't seen anything out of the ordinary, that he knew everyone who was dressed in black. And Frances wasn't on the guest list, unless of course, he had been using a different name.

"No, the poor man," Eleanor said in even tones. "The news didn't even give out his name that night, although it did the following day."

"Was he shot?" Francis asked.

He addressed the question to me, but I looked at the sisters. I didn't want to say the wrong thing.

Thankfully, Matilda spoke up. "No, the doctor who attended to him told Jane she saw a needle mark in his neck."

"She thought he had been poisoned," I said.

Frances spread a thick layer of butter on his bread roll. "Imagine that, somebody hating you enough to want to kill you in front of a room full of witnesses." He turned to slap Damon on the shoulder. "But we have seen some strange things in our line of work, haven't we!"

"We certainly have."

"But Damon, you haven't answered my original question yet. Are you close to solving the murder?"

Damon shook his head. "I was taken off the case on account of my broken ankle."

"Oh yes, of course you would have been. Still, you must be in close contact with the detectives on the case. Have they solved it yet?"

Damon shrugged. "They haven't been in contact with me at all. I suppose they want me to rest. Besides, those detectives aren't close friends of mine, so they have no reason to fill me in on the details. It's not as if I started the case. I injured myself after a few minutes, and the detective who was with me at the time, Detective Green, had to go out of town because he had new evidence on a cold case he'd worked years ago."

The conversation turned to Matilda and Eleanor's goats. I only half-listened, because I wondered why Francis was so interested in the case. It certainly concerned me.

After dessert, ice cream with salted pretzels, I offered to drive Damon to Rebecca's. After all, he looked horribly tired. "That would be lovely, thanks Jane," he said.

"And I'll take you wherever you want to go, Frances."

"That's very kind of you," Frances began, but Matilda interrupted him.

"I'll drive Frances home later," she said. "That is, if you don't mind me borrowing your car, Jane?"

"That's okay. It *is* insured," I said, alarmed. "Just be careful, won't you?"

"I always am," Matilda said with a smile.

I knew she was up to something. I just didn't know what it was, and I could hardly ask in front of Damon and Frances.

Frances and I helped Damon to the car. He

kept telling us he was all right and to stop fussing, but I think he secretly liked the attention. Once in the car, it was quite a short drive to Rebecca's. I grabbed my flashlight from the car and went to help Damon, but he was already out of the car and on his crutches. "I'll be all right, Jane," he protested.

I watched as he made his way to the porch steps. "Maybe I need some help now," he said with a laugh.

At the top of the stairs and on the porch, I opened the door and helped Damon inside. "Can you manage from here?" I asked him.

He pulled me into his arms and kissed me thoroughly by way of response.

CHAPTER 16

I leaned back in my chair, exhausted. "I've managed to exclude most of the people from the volunteer list and the guest list. That is, I've eliminated them if they are under the age of eighty," I said.

Eleanor looked over my shoulder. She was holding Mr. Crumbles, and he took a playful swipe at me. "How did you do that?" she asked me.

"By their social media," I said.

Eleanor nodded her approval. "And remember to make a note of people who are not on social media. That's suspicious."

"It most certainly is not suspicious to avoid social media!" Matilda said tersely. "Many nice, normal people do not have social media."

Eleanor sighed long and hard. "I meant in this context, Matilda. Context is important. The Raven isn't likely to have social media accounts, is he? Who would he have for friends? The prison guards? Other criminals? And what would he post about? People he has assassinated? How many Likes do you think that would get?" She put her hands on her hips and glowered at Matilda.

Matilda ignored her. "So, Jane, who do we have?"

"Nobody! Nobody, only Silas Greeves and Marvin were over the age of eighty."

"What about the guest list?"

"The only people over eighty on the guest list were women."

Matilda nodded. "We need to question Wanda."

"Wanda?" I repeated in surprise. I swiveled around in my office chair to face her. "Didn't you say we didn't need to know which poison the Raven used? That knowing the poison wouldn't help us to track him down?"

Matilda pursed her lips and looked none too pleased. "Yes, you are right. I *did* indeed say that, but the two remarks are not mutually exclusive."

"I don't understand."

"In order to avoid being seen as acting suspiciously, we need to follow our usual routine in our investigations."

For once, Eleanor agreed with her. "And our usual routine is visiting Wanda and asking her questions."

"That makes sense," I admitted.

Matilda nodded. "And who knows, Wanda might be able to give us some pertinent information."

"Will all three of us go?" I asked. "Shouldn't somebody stay here on guard? Just in case Dr. Ramsgate is the Raven, because if he is, he's already suspicious of the two of you."

"We have plenty of surveillance equipment around," Eleanor said dismissively. She pulled up her long skirt to show a red lace garter on her thigh. In it was a revolver.

I sat there, shocked.

Eleanor pushed on. "We are fully armed," she said. "I'm wearing other weapons on my person."

I clamped my hand firmly over my eyes. "That's all well and good, but please don't feel you have to show them to me. And where's Frances? When I went to bed last night, he was still here, and you were all talking."

The sisters exchanged glances.

"I drove him home," Matilda said. "After he had a problem with his medication," she added.

Eleanor sniggered. "A *big* problem."

Soon, the three of us had made our way past Billy unscathed, and I was driving in the direction of Wanda's house. Wanda lived in a *grossmammi haus* behind the main house where her daughter, Waneta, and Waneta's husband lived. Waneta did filing for the coroner's office, and that had come in handy in the past.

Eleanor leaned over between the driver's seat and the passenger seat. "I hope Wanda is home."

"She is," I said, gesturing to the paddock on my left. "That's her buggy horse there."

Matilda craned her neck to look at the bay horse. "You do have a good eye, Jane. All horses look the same to me."

I chuckled and brought the car to a stop outside Wanda's front fence. A white paling fence surrounded the *grossmammi haus,* and the garden held all manner of medicinal herbs as well as culinary herbs. Of course, most herbs had a dual purpose, as I well knew from being raised Amish.

Matilda and Eleanor likewise took a great interest in herbs.

"Wanda has a wonderful herb collection," Eleanor gushed as she looked over the fence. "That's the healthiest goldenseal I've ever seen!"

"Get a grip, Eleanor," Matilda snapped. "We have those same herbs at home."

"But we have been neglecting them," Eleanor reminded her. "This has spurred me on to get our herb garden going nicely again."

"Good for you," Matilda mumbled.

"I read only the other day that goldenseal has strong anti-aging properties," Eleanor continued. "It's lucky I've been taking it for years."

"Clearly, you need a stronger dose," Matilda muttered.

I hoped their bickering wouldn't escalate, but to my relief, Wanda flung the front door open. "*Wunderbar!*" she exclaimed. "I was wondering why I hadn't seen the three of you lately, what with you being involved in another murder and all."

Wanda held the door ajar and beckoned us inside. I handed her a basket, in which were several stuffed cabbage rolls as well as a variety of cupcakes: pumpkin pie cupcakes, soft molasses cupcakes, banana bread cupcakes, caramel apple coffee cupcakes.

"*Denki*, Jane. You usually come for breakfast,"

she added with a chuckle. "I don't have any scrapple left."

"Oh, that's all right," Matilda said, but Wanda held up one hand to forestall her.

"I do have potato salad, and I was about to make haystacks."

Eleanor looked alarmed. "Haystacks? But isn't that food for goats?"

The rest of us laughed. Even Matilda laughed, although she followed her laughter by, "Eleanor, you know very well what haystacks are. You have had them before."

"I think I'd remember if I had." Eleanor pulled a face.

Matilda rolled her eyes. "You start with corn chips or crackers, then add a base of rice or noodles. After that, you add the meat sauce, then anything you like, such as lettuce, tomatoes, peppers, beans, onions, and then top it with cheese."

"Why didn't you say so?" Eleanor said.

Wanda ushered us into the kitchen. "Sit down. *Kaffi?*"

"Yes, please," I said. I rarely refused coffee.

Matilda and Eleanor opted instead for hot meadow tea.

Soon, the aroma of fragrant peppermint permeated the kitchen. "I'm surprised you have taken so long," Wanda said. "Since you were there with the victim when he died, Jane, I expected to see you the very next morning or maybe the morning after, but now, several days have passed." She frowned so deeply that her eyebrows formed a unibrow.

I didn't know what to say, so simply sat there, smiling and nodding. I felt foolish, but I didn't know what story to tell her.

Thankfully, Matilda had no such problem. "Well, Jane's friend, Damon, Detective Damon McCloud, that is, injured himself at the art gallery when attending the scene of the crime, and broke his ankle. He was taken to the hospital, and our time has been taken visiting him in the hospital. Now, he is staying with Rebecca and Ephraim for a few days."

Wanda nodded. "*Jah*, I knew that."

Of course, she did. It was a small community after all, and news traveled fast.

Wanda pushed on. "Well, aren't you going to ask me?"

"Ask you what?" I countered.

Wanda threw up both hands, palms to the ceiling. "Why, what the poison was, of course!"

Eleanor leaned forward. "Oh yes, we've been absolutely consumed with curiosity, haven't we Matilda?"

Matilda, too, leaned across the table. "Yes, but we didn't think they'd know by now, since it was clearly such a fast-acting poison. If we thought they'd know by now, we would have come sooner, wouldn't we, Eleanor?"

Eleanor nodded solemnly. "We would indeed."

"And do you know what the poison is?" I prompted Wanda.

She looked quite pleased with herself. "*Jah*, Waneta told me and asked me to tell you. It was ricin."

"Ricin?" I echoed.

Matilda pulled a face. "The poor man, what a way to go." To me, she said, "Ricin powder the size of a few grains of salt will kill a person quickly. It's a highly potent poison."

Eleanor added to the explanation. "It's far more deadly injected or inhaled than it is when ingested."

"It was certainly a fast-acting poison, that's for

sure," I said. "He didn't have time to call for help after the murderer injected it into him."

"Actually, ricin usually takes a few days to kill a victim," Matilda added. "That suggests the concentration in the injection was high. Wanda, did Waneta mention how they were able to discover it was ricin so quickly?"

Wanda shrugged. "She said they were looking for very fast acting poisons. Like you said, Jane, the man didn't have time to call out for help. Waneta specifically mentioned they said that. They knew it had to be something that could act that quickly and apparently, that narrowed it down."

Matilda nodded. "Yes, despite what you see on TV, there are not many poisons which act that quickly. The ones that spring to mind are cyanide, thallium, batrachotoxin, tetrodotoxin, certain nerve gases, and maybe one or two others."

"But Matilda, Wanda doesn't watch television. She's Amish, if you hadn't noticed."

Matilda rounded on Eleanor. "I didn't say Wanda watches television. I didn't say Wanda *has* a television. What are you talking about, Eleanor?"

"You said it wasn't like what she saw on TV." Eleanor pouted.

"I was speaking in general terms."

"Wet-bottom Shoo-fly pie?" Wanda spoke loudly and stood up abruptly. I was glad that she asked because it broke up the argument. She crossed to the fridge and brought out a large pie. In no time, she had cut it into slices.

"Don't forget the cupcakes we brought," I reminded her.

"We can have both," Wanda said with a laugh.

I laughed, too. "You won't get any argument from me." I thought about how hospitable the Amish were. People could turn up unannounced, any time of the day or night, and the Amish would always feed them.

As soon as we left, I wasted no time questioning the sisters about ricin. "It's a particularly *spy* type of poison?" I asked them.

"No," they both said in unison.

Matilda explained further. "Despite it being such a deadly poison, ricin is quite easy to make. It's in the shells of castor oil beans, so if anybody chews castor oil beans, then they become very ill indeed."

"But nobody chews the shells of castor oil beans," Eleanor pointed out.

"Eleanor is right," Matilda said with a frown. "Nobody *does* chew the shells of castor oil beans, which is why there are not plenty of poisoned people lying about."

"So, it's of no help to the investigation?" I asked.

"No," Matilda said firmly. "As I said, there are not many poisons that could have killed Scarface so quickly. The Raven would have access to all of them, so simply finding out the type of poison was of no help whatsoever to us. We knew that. Still, it was good that we visited Wanda, as that is something we normally do."

Eleanor piped up from the back seat. "Even Wanda said she was surprised we hadn't gone there earlier."

"Yes," I said absently. "What do we do now?"

"We find the Raven," Matilda said solemnly. "We find the Raven, before the Raven finds us."

CHAPTER 17

I was concerned we weren't getting anywhere with the case. I said as much to Matilda and Eleanor. We were all driving to speak with Mrs. Cindy Bellamy, Dr. Ramsgate's former secretary. I had no idea whether we would get any pertinent information from her, but so far, we had hit a brick wall with the investigation. At least, that's how it seemed to me.

"After all this is over, I will invite Frances to join us for dinner," Eleanor announced out of the blue.

Matilda spun around to look at her. "Why?" she shrieked.

"I'm trying a bit of matchmaking," Eleanor said. "I know you like him."

"Don't be ridiculous," Matilda snapped. "I simply find him entertaining, that's all."

"Then you will find him entertaining at dinner." To me, she said, "I hope you don't mind, Jane?"

"Not at all. It's your home as much as it is mine. Oh, and something occurred to me in the middle of last night when I woke up and couldn't get back to sleep. You don't think Frances is the Raven, do you? I mean, he's about the right age. Don't you think it's suspicious that he booked himself into the hospital just after the murder? And there was nothing wrong with him, according to the nurse, but he ended up in the same ward as Damon because he faked the same type of injury. And then he got in the trunk of my car."

"Yes, that did occur to us too," Matilda said.

"Then why didn't you tell me?"

"We didn't want to worry you, of course."

"But why did you invite him to my house?"

"We wanted to see if he was the Raven," Matilda said. "We have our ways."

I was puzzled. "What do you mean?"

"I mean, we found out he isn't the Raven. We asked him, and he said he wasn't."

I was exasperated. "I can't believe you used to

be a spy! And what about all the questions he asked at dinner? You're simply taking his word for it?"

"Of course," Eleanor piped up.

"But what makes you think he was telling the truth?"

"Because we drugged him with an updated version of SP-17," Eleanor told me. "We gave him a decent dose. He wasn't able to lie."

I did not know how to respond. I went cold all over. "Do you mean to tell me that you drugged Frances and gave him some sort of a truth serum in order to ask him if he was the Raven?"

"There's no such thing as a truth serum, really," Eleanor said solemnly. "It simply makes one suggestible and relieves anxiety and tension. It...."

Eleanor had no chance to finish her sentence. "That's not the point!" I said shrilly. "You drugged an innocent person?"

"We didn't know he was an innocent person at the time," Matilda pointed out. "For all we knew, it was him or us. Besides, we didn't harm him, did we, Eleanor?"

"Not at all. And we tied him down with furry handcuffs so they wouldn't hurt him. But there's no need to worry, the drug erases any memory of the event."

"I've heard enough!" I all but screamed. "I don't want to hear another word!" Nanoseconds later, I said, "And where did all this happen?"

I shot a glance in the rear vision mirror at Matilda to see her smirking at me. "I thought you said you didn't want to hear another word."

I scowled at her, so she quickly added, "In the basement, of course."

"The basement?" I squealed.

"You said we could have that room to do whatever we wanted. You said it could be our very own space."

"Yes, but I didn't think you were going to torture people down there."

"We didn't torture him," Eleanor said. "But Jane, you're missing the point. Frances isn't the Raven, after all. Everything you said was right. We *were* highly suspicious of him. He checked himself into the hospital with a fake injury. He made friends with Damon. He stole your car. That was a perfect opportunity to put a surveillance device in it. The fact we didn't find one made it no less suspicious. He hid in the trunk of your car. He asked too many questions at

CONFECTIONS OF A PARTYGOER

dinner. To all outward appearances, he was a funny, friendly person. All that made us suspicious."

"Eleanor's right," Matilda said. "He had gotten too close. We had to find out if he was the Raven, and when he was in the house, and when you were safely asleep, we had a good opportunity to interrogate him."

"Well, that's just great," I said sarcastically.

The sisters murmured their agreement.

I rolled my eyes and concentrated on driving. I tried to calm myself by taking long, slow, deep breaths. It seemed to work a little.

Mrs. Cindy Bellamy lived in a small house on the outskirts of town. As I cut the engine, something occurred to me. I voiced my concerns aloud. "Can you be sure the Raven isn't a woman?"

Both sisters stared at me as though I had gone mad. "Of course not!" they said in unison.

I waved my finger at them. "But think about it. You wanted the Raven to believe that you were men the whole time, so why isn't it possible that he's actually a woman? And if that's the case, then this Cindy Bellamy might be the Raven."

"But don't forget, the Raven was incarcerated

for decades," Matilda told me. "Somebody would have noticed if he was a woman in all that time."

I slapped my palm on my forehead. "Of course! I feel foolish."

It was Matilda's turn to wave her finger at me. "Not at all, Jane. Rather than foolish, that was a very clever thing to say. It shows you're thinking outside of the box. Now, do you have your story straight for this woman?"

I nodded. "Yes, been there, done that. I've told the same story to a few people already."

There was a sign on Mrs. Bellamy's door that asked people not to ring the bell. I wondered if knocking was permitted. Matilda, however, had no such qualms, as she knocked loudly on the door. I at once heard footsteps shuffling to the door.

A friendly-faced woman opened it. She had tight, curly, white hair and an abundance of wrinkles over her face. "Hello?"

"I'm Jane Delight, and these are my friends, Matilda and Eleanor," I told her. "I hope you don't mind, but I would like to ask you some questions about the art gallery."

"The art gallery?" she repeated.

I nodded. Matilda took over the conversation.

"You might have heard there was a murder the other night at the art gallery?"

Mrs. Bellamy nodded.

"Have you heard from Dr. Ramsgate lately?"

She shook her head. "I haven't heard from him in years."

Matilda nodded. "Dr. Ramsgate and my friend, Jane, here have been investigating. The police haven't made any headway in that case, and Dr. Ramsgate is afraid he won't be able to have another exhibition until the murder is solved. Violet Peavesbody suggested we contact you."

"Violet! Oh yes, such a lovely woman. Yes, that makes sense. Having a murder on the premises would affect the business. Would you like to come in?"

We thanked her and walked inside. There was a large white plastic gate in front of us, blocking our way. "Mind the cat doesn't get out," she said. She slammed the plastic gate behind us, and the cat, a pretty ginger and white, scurried away.

Mrs. Bellamy showed us into the living room and told us to sit on the couch. She sat on another couch, one at right angles to the one on which I was sitting. The cat reappeared and jumped onto her lap. I looked around the room. It looked cozy and would have felt quite small but for the high, raked ceilings. The room was awfully dark, with the curtains drawn and only one corner lamp providing the rather scant, yellowing illumination.

"Would you like some coffee?"

We all said that we would. The home was split level, rather an unusual design, and the kitchen countertop was set a little higher than the living room. From there, Cindy Bellamy was able to look over the edge at us. She continued speaking while she was making the coffee. "Are all you ladies private detectives?"

"Jane is," Eleanor said, as quick as a flash. "Matilda and I are her assistants."

"It must be a very exciting life," Mrs. Bellamy said.

"Sometimes *too* exciting," I told her.

Soon, we were all sitting and sipping coffee. The smell of mold and dampness hung in the air. I wondered why I hadn't noticed it until now.

"What questions would you like to ask me?" she said. "I don't know if I can be of any help, because I haven't worked at the art gallery for years."

"How many years ago did you retire?" I asked her.

"It was four years ago," she said. "One of the volunteers suggested to Dr. Ramsgate that the volunteers could do the work I did and said he didn't need to employ me any longer."

"That doesn't seem very fair," Matilda said.

She shook her head and then nodded. "No, but I did get paid rather a lot of money to leave. I was well and truly past retirement age by then, and I was only staying on at the art gallery because I thought there was nobody else to do my job. When I realized the volunteers could do the work I was doing, I was more than happy to leave. In fact, I would have left years earlier if I could have."

"Was there one volunteer in particular who said you should leave?" I asked her.

"Yes, but I've forgotten his name. He was new at the time, you see. A tall man with a white beard. He looked awfully like Dr. Ramsgate. He's Violet's neighbor."

"Silas Greeves?" I prompted her.

She clapped her hands twice. "Yes, that's him! A rather unpleasant man. although do forgive me for saying so."

"In what way is he unpleasant?" Eleanor asked her.

"I worked at the gallery for years with Henry

Hickman, the director before Dr. Ramsgate came. Henry was a lovely man, and when Dr. Ramsgate first came, he was nice and friendly too. Not that he was very sociable, mind you. He was a loner. Around the time that Silas Greeves arrived, Dr. Ramsgate became even more withdrawn and less friendly."

"Did it happen suddenly or over a period of time?" Eleanor asked her.

She shrugged. "I can't remember. Does it matter? Anyway, he was still nice enough to his staff. But, you see, Dr. Ramsgate wasn't a people person. He didn't even like pets." She stroked her cat. "Said he was allergic to cats. I mean, who knows if that was true? But he didn't have so much as a goldfish. No, all he cared about were his plants. Once he told me if he hadn't been in his line of work, he would have been a botanist. Obsessed with his plants, he was. What a shame he wasn't more of a people person. And then that Silas Greeves. He was even less of a people person."

"Can you tell me any more about Silas Greeves?"

She appeared to be thinking it over. "No, not really. Only that he pretended to be frail, and he always complained about his bad back, but once I saw him sprinting along the street to beat a younger man to a taxi."

"And did you know Marvin Maze?"

She looked up at me in surprise. "The man who was murdered?"

I nodded.

"No, I had never met him. I hadn't even heard of him, to be honest, not until I heard about him on the news."

"He was a volunteer," I told her.

"Must've been after my time," she said. "Sometimes I miss it, you know, the art gallery and the hustle and bustle, but I'm quite happy living here with my husband and my cat."

"I didn't know you had a husband," I said.

She pointed in the direction of the window. "He's in the garden. He's a keen gardener."

"Thanks for your help and for the coffee," I told her.

Matilda thanked her too. "And Mrs. Bellamy, please don't mention to anybody that we were here. We have to be discreet in our line of work."

"I understand perfectly." She showed us to the door and cautioned us once more not to let the cat through the white plastic gate.

CHAPTER 18

"Are you sure this is the theme?" Matilda stuck her head around my bathroom door. "England?"

"That's exactly what it says on the invitation." I stared at the thick white card and studied the cursive writing. "It says, *You are hereby invited to Dr. Ramsgate's Fundraising Costume Ball. The theme is England. Your costume should reflect this theme.* I don't think it could be a typo."

"I don't know anything about the English," Matilda said thoughtfully. "What do I know about the English?"

"But you *are* English," I said, puzzled.

"Please Jane, I have to stay in character." Matilda stepped into my bathroom. "Ask Damon."

"Why would I ask Damon?" Damon and I were attending the event together. Maybe I should have asked him earlier what costume he intended to wear so we could match.

"He's Scottish."

Matilda mumbled something and left. I placed the invitation on the counter and picked up a brush, sweeping it over the powder blush.

I had decided to go as Queen Elizabeth. I had always admired her colorful matching skirt suits, but until I began researching her style for the fundraising ball, I had not known she wore bright colors so people in the crowds could spot her.

I also had not known she had worn the same brand of loafers for the last fifty years. I didn't own a pair of loafers, but I did own a pair of sneakers that looked as though they had been worn for the last fifty years. I am not sure Her Majesty would have approved, but I did not have the money to buy anything else.

As for my matching skirt suit, I'd picked a daring shade of lime green. I had also managed to find a short, white wig. The hat I would have to go without, but that would not matter.

"Matilda," I called out. "Eleanor. Are you ready to go?"

I took one last look at myself in the mirror. I did look quite a bit like the Queen in my matching lime green skirt suit. I stepped from the bathroom and dropped my purse. Eleanor was wearing a Union Jack mini dress with platform boots, while Matilda was wearing a tracksuit with a fake tattoo drawn onto her arm. At least, I hoped it was a fake tattoo.

"What on earth?" I said.

"Eleanor had a good idea—for once—about the theme of the ball," Matilda said. "The Spice Girls were English!"

"They probably still are," I replied, because I was too stunned to say anything else. "Eleanor, isn't that mini dress a bit too, um, *mini*?"

"I'm Ginger Spice," Eleanor explained. "Do you remember when she wore that famous Union Jack mini dress? Apparently, they were so afraid of being disrespectful by using an actual Union Jack flag, they cut up a Union Jack dish towel instead. Isn't that fascinating?"

I gulped. "Fascinating is one word for all of this. Matilda, when are you getting ready for the ball? Damon will be here any minute."

"I *am* ready," Matilda replied. "I am Sporty Spice."

"Okay," I said. I was dismayed. I had one housemate horribly underdressed and one housemate horribly overdressed. Just when I thought things couldn't get any worse, they did. "Um, Eleanor, what are you doing with Mr. Crumbles?"

"This is Baby Spice, actually." Eleanor picked up Mr. Crumbles. He was wearing a diaper.

"I don't think Baby Spice ran around on stage in a diaper, Eleanor," I said. "I'm sorry, but Mr. Crumbles will have to stay here and guard the house. Come on, you two. We have to get Damon."

"Why are you wearing sneakers, Jane?" Eleanor asked. "It doesn't suit the rest of your wonderful outfit."

"I'm wearing loafers."

"You're wearing sneakers," Eleanor corrected. "And why aren't you in costume?"

"I *am* in costume. When have you ever seen me wear a lime green skirt suit?"

Eleanor looked me up and down. "I thought you had finally decided to be stylish. Your hair is looking a lot better too."

I sighed. Tonight was going to be a very long night. "Come on, then. Let's go get Damon. I bet he absolutely hates the idea of a fundraising costume ball. I bet he's miserable the whole time. I bet he doesn't even wear a costume, and we'll all look like crazy people standing next to him."

Matilda, Eleanor, and I locked up the house and stepped outside. I shrieked when I saw my car. It had been painted to resemble a double-decker bus with the Union Jack painted on the side.

Matilda hurried to reassure me. "It's water-based paint," she said. "You can wash it off tomorrow."

"*You* can wash it off tomorrow," I countered.

"All aboard the Spice Bus," Eleanor cried out.

I shook my head.

When we reached Rebecca's house moments later, I got out of the car and walked up the stairs. Damon flung open the front door.

I gasped so hard I nearly fell backward down the stairs.

Damon was wearing a leopard print leotard, and he had leopard ears pinned onto his head.

"Damon!" I exclaimed. "What are you wearing?"

"I'm Scary Spice," Damon said, and suddenly he sounded a little defensive. "The theme is England?"

"I don't think English people wear leopard print leotards, Damon," I said.

"And if they do," Matilda replied, "they really shouldn't."

"Eleanor said we were all going as the Spice Girls." Damon looked over my shoulder. "Where is Baby Spice?"

"Mean old Jane wouldn't let Mr. Crumbles come to the ball," Eleanor told him.

"We can't be the Spice Girls without Baby Spice, and Jane, I thought you were going as Posh Spice."

"I forgot to tell her we had decided on a group costume," Eleanor admitted. "I forgot to tell Matilda too, but thankfully I already had her costume ready to go. Should we all get on the Spice Bus then?"

Damon turned to me. "Why aren't you wearing a costume?"

"Ha ha, very funny." I scowled at him. "Let's just get going."

Damon kissed me on the cheek. "I love what you've done with your hair."

Frowning, I stepped onboard the Spice Bus. Eleanor was muttering from the back seat. "Whatever happened to the days when a man arrived appropriately in a limousine? He would wear a suit, and he would introduce himself to your father."

"That never happened. You're dreaming," Matilda snapped at her.

We arrived at the ball, which was being held at the private estate owned by one of Dr. Smythe's' friends, and left the Spice Bus.

The other guests had gone all out with the theme. In the first five minutes, I spotted The Beatles, three Mary Poppins, eleven Chimney Sweeps, five kings, seven royal guards in the red uniforms with those tall black hats, and one Prince William.

"Hello, Granny." He kissed me on the cheek.

After he left, Damon turned to me with a frown. "I know Dr. Ramsgate said to make ourselves feel comfortable," he said, "but I don't think he meant us to make ourselves *that* comfortable."

"He *is* my grandson, Damon." I elbowed him in the ribs.

I did enjoy how attentive Damon was to me. It did, however, mean I needed to be a little tricky when I did things I did not want him to know I was doing, like scanning the room for the Raven.

"Looking for someone?"

A chill trickled up my spine. It was Silas. Silas Greeves. He was dressed as Prince Charming, complete with a cape and a fake sword. At least, I hoped the sword was fake.

"I only ask because you are skulking around like a little mouse," Silas added, with an unpleasant smirk.

"Do mouses skulk?" I asked.

"Evidently, this one does."

"I like your costume," I lied. I didn't know what else to say to Silas.

"There is no need to lie," Silas said. He loomed over me. "I don't have feelings, but even if I did, I doubt you could hurt them."

"Jane?" A familiar voice said.

I turned and found Eleanor at my side.

Matilda joined us and added, "Are you okay?"

"Yes, I was just talking to Silas here," I replied, but when I turned back, Silas Greeves had disappeared. "That's funny."

"What do you think about him?" Matilda whispered to me.

"Nothing good," I replied. "He didn't seem so mean when we last met him."

If only I was as tall as Silas, I would not have

needed to stand on my toes to try to find Dr. Ramsgate at the ball. I did think it was the polite thing to do to thank him for the invitation, but for the life of me, I could not guess which costume he would be wearing. I doubted he was a Mary Poppins or a Chimney Sweep. There was a little orphan Oliver Twist rattling a tin, but he seemed too short to be the good doctor.

Damon hobbled over to me on his crutches. "Hide me. I'm far too magnetic as Scary Spice, and the women won't leave me alone."

"You poor thing," I said sarcastically. I looked at him and was concerned to see his face was pale. "Are you in pain?"

"Oh, I don't know," he said dismissively. "Maybe a twinge or two."

"Let us get Matilda and Eleanor and leave. We'll miss the auction of local goods, but I don't think any of us have the money to spare." *And we haven't discovered anything of use here anyway*, I silently added.

"No, not after I blew it all on this costume."

Giggling, I took Damon by the hand and we went off to find Matilda and Eleanor. It was not long before the four of us, three Spice Girls and the Queen of England, were exiting through the front doors of the mansion.

Even though I had spent my time at the ball looking for him, I had not seen Dr. Ramsgate all night. It was not until now, with proceedings winding down, and the gravel driveway outside the grand old house peppered with partygoers and the cars sent to retrieve them, that I saw him. He stood on the first-floor balcony, his eyes silver in the moonlight, staring down at the people like Gatsby looking across the bay at the green light at the end of Daisy Buchanan's dock. I do not know what he searched for in the night. I could only hope that the murder which had brought us together would not end in the same tragedy as *The Great Gatsby*.

And with that sobering thought, I boarded the Spice Bus.

CHAPTER 19

I'd had a terrible night's sleep. I had tossed and turned, and had most likely been grinding my teeth, given the fact that my jaw was horribly sore when I awoke.

I hurried down to the kitchen to make coffee and counted the seconds before Matilda and Eleanor surfaced.

"Good morning," they said in unison.

"I think you were right, Eleanor," I said.

Both Matilda and Eleanor appeared shocked.

"Eleanor? Right about what?" Matilda's mouth formed a perfect *O*.

"When Eleanor said a body could be hidden in sarcophagi."

"It's sarcophaguses, not sarcophagi," Matilda corrected me. "It's derived from an ancient Greek third declension word, so it should be *sarcophaguses*. If it were a Latin word, it would be sarcophagi, only it isn't a Latin word, it's a Greek word."

"Err, okay," I said, my head spinning.

"But Eleanor, bodies were always in sarcophaguses," Matilda added.

"Jane means a *modern* murdered body," Eleanor told her. "Don't you remember what I said?"

Matilda shrugged. "I most likely do remember what you said, but I have no idea what you're talking about, as usual."

I hurried to explain. "We were wondering whether Dr. Ramsgate could be the murderer. We discussed the possibility of him stealing the identity of the real Dr. Ramsgate, but we concluded that it would be too risky a thing to do because if the real Dr. Ramsgate's body turned up, his cover would be blown."

"I remember that discussion perfectly well," Matilda said. "What of it?"

I had already had my first cup of coffee, so I poured coffee into the sisters' cups. "Eleanor said a sarcophagus would be a good place to hide a body."

"A *modern* murder victim," Eleanor added.

Matilda's face lit up. "I see! And that lady at the ball last night said that Dr. Ramsgate used to be the curator of a museum of antiquities. Did she mention Egyptian artifacts?"

"What lady?" I exclaimed. "You didn't tell me about a lady!"

"I didn't want to worry you," Matilda said, "and I *am* telling you now."

Eleanor shook her head. "No, she didn't, and I couldn't find any mention of Dr. Ramsgate been associated with that museum online, but I did google the museum, and it does have Egyptian antiquities."

"You might be onto something, Jane," Matilda said. "I thought it was Dr. Ramsgate all along."

Eleanor disagreed with her. "No, you didn't. You only think that now because the evidence is pointing to him."

Matilda's face turned beet red. I spoke quickly. "So, we should all go to the museum and find out if they have a sarcophagus. Maybe look inside it."

Eleanor shook her head. "I was undercover years ago at the University of Manchester in England, and they have a prestigious Egyptology section. There is no way they will open a sarcophagus in anything less than a specially controlled environment."

"Maybe they have a specially controlled environment at this museum," I offered.

Eleanor shook her head vehemently. "Absolutely not. It takes a huge amount of funding to provide such an environment."

I threw up my hands, palms to the ceiling. "So then, what do we do?"

Matilda and Eleanor exchanged glances. Mr. Crumbles walked into the room, yawned, and stretched. Eleanor at once hurried to pour food into his bowl. He followed her, meowing loudly.

When no answer was forthcoming, I said, "We need to visit this museum. Maybe the curator or a member of staff can tell us something about Dr. Ramsgate. If we get enough information, maybe we can tell everything to the detectives on the case, and they can look inside the sarcophagus."

"No!" Matilda exclaimed.

Eleanor looked up from stroking Mr. Crumbles and added, "No!"

Matilda was the one who offered the explanation. "We can't get involved, Jane. We can't do anything that could compromise our identities.

If anything, we will make an anonymous tip-off to the police, but first, we have to be certain that Dr. Ramsgate is, in fact, the Raven, and that the original Dr. Ramsgate's body is in the sarcophagus."

"It's Sunday today, so Rebecca's store is shut for the day."

"What about Damon? Will he get in our way?" Matilda asked me.

I shook my head. "No, because Rebecca and Ephraim won't be going to the meeting today as it's the off week. Damon said he's going to spend time with them today."

Eleanor stopped stroking Mr. Crumbles. "There's a meeting?"

Matilda rounded on her. "Goodness me, Eleanor, have the bats flown off with your wits?"

"What bats?"

Matilda pouted. "Exactly! Eleanor, you very well know that the Amish refer to the church service in their homes as meetings, and that the church service is every other week. They're not going to their meeting today, so I assume Damon feels he should spend some time with them to thank them for their hospitality."

"I know that," Eleanor snapped.

"I googled the museum, and it's open on Sundays," I told them. "Shall we go first thing this morning?"

Matilda took some time to answer. "No, because if Dr. Ramsgate has eyes on us, he'll know the gig is up. We need to separate."

I was puzzled. "What do you mean?"

Matilda broke some stale bread into her bowl of coffee. "The Raven might be suspicious of us, but we have no idea whether that's the case. To be on the safe side, the three of us should split up. Maybe you can take me somewhere, Jane, and take Eleanor somewhere else. Then you should sit at a café for a time before going to the museum. The Raven won't be able to follow all three of us, and you're the least likely person he will want to follow. The Raven is after the two of us, after all."

I nodded slowly. "That makes sense."

Matilda pushed on. "You can take me to a shopping mall, and maybe take Eleanor to a gym."

Eleanor shrieked. "I want to go to a shopping mall! I don't want to go to a gym."

"Why don't I take you to a shopping mall, Matilda, and Eleanor, I can take you to a different shopping mall?"

Matilda shook her head. "That won't do at all. The Raven would at once be suspicious as to why we didn't go together."

I looked at Eleanor. "Why don't I take you to a café? You can eat cake?"

Matilda tapped her chin. "No, that won't work. The Raven would still be suspicious because the two of us could go to the same shopping mall and have coffee later."

I was running out of options. A heavy silence fell upon us for a few moments, broken only when Eleanor finally snapped, "All right! I'll go to a gym."

I was glad the matter was settled. After a hearty breakfast, I got dressed and met the sisters downstairs.

"Remember, Jane, be very careful," Eleanor warned me. "Maybe you should take a weapon."

"Weapons are dangerous when somebody doesn't know how to use them," Matilda countered.

"I'm not going to take a weapon, but I do have my phone, and I can text you as soon as I find out any information," I told them. I was relieved they hadn't suggested I wear a wire again.

That seemed to make them both happy. I drove

Matilda to a shopping mall, driving slightly slower than usual to give the Raven an opportunity to follow me through traffic, and then I drove Eleanor a distance away to a gym. "Don't forget to text as soon as you have some information," she reminded me.

I assured her that I would. I then drove in the opposite direction to the museum to a small café. I parked and went inside. To my delight, there was a spare table near the window. I sat there and ordered a Dirty Chai Latte and a large slice of Peanut Butter Pie.

There were few other patrons in the café, and I carefully watched anybody who came in. Nobody was over the age of eighty, and I certainly didn't see any sign of Dr. Ramsgate, Silas Greeves, or Dr. Smythe for that matter. Likewise, nobody I spied through the window fitted those descriptions.

I pulled my phone out of my purse and looked at the time. I was anxious, worried that the Raven had followed me. Still, I knew Matilda was right—he would be more likely to follow one of the sisters. After all, they were his prey.

I shuddered and shook myself. I went over to pay and then left, doing my best not to look around me. As I drove away, I continually looked in the rear vision mirror, but I couldn't see anybody following me. Still, the traffic would have camouflaged anybody who was hard on my tail.

I drove to the museum and easily found somewhere to park. Once more, I stood and looked around me, but no other cars had followed me. I took that as a good sign. I took a deep breath, silently urged myself on, and headed for the front door of the museum.

I paid the lady at the entrance, and she shoved a brochure into my hands. I stood aside a little to look through the brochure. The current exhibition was a Greek and Roman exhibition of mosaics, bronze statues and reliefs, as well as bronze statuettes. There was no mention of anything Egyptian.

I decided to walk around and look at the exhibition. Maybe something would come to light. If it didn't, I intended to question a staff member.

As I walked past the Attic red-figure drinking cups, a statue of Medusa, and rows of pottery shards from different time periods, I kept one eye on the door for one of the suspects.

However, that was not possible when I went into the adjoining rooms, but I made sure I popped back from time to time to check out anybody who had just entered.

After fifteen minutes, I had seen plenty of pottery and statues, but all the other patrons were clearly under the age of eighty. I certainly hoped that if the Raven was following anybody, he wasn't following me.

I had only seen one staff member to date, the lady at the front desk. I approached her. "Excuse me."

She looked up, a smile on her face. "Can I help you?"

"Yes, I'm an associate of Dr. Reginald Ramsgate. I believe he used to be the curator here."

She bit her lip. "I'm sorry, I have no idea. When was this?"

"Around ten years or so ago," I told her.

She smiled and nodded. "I've only been working here a few months."

"I see. Well, I've come here today to speak to somebody about the Egyptian exhibition."

"Oh, we haven't had any Egyptian exhibitions in ages," she said. "That much I do know."

I waved one hand at her. "Sorry, I worded that

wrongly. I believe you have Egyptian artifacts in storage."

"Yes, that's right, we do."

"I wanted to know if you have a sarcophagus."

"Oh, I've never looked back out there," she said.

This was going nowhere. "Is there anybody here today I could ask?" I prompted her.

"Yes, Dr. Andersen is here today. Would you like to speak with him?"

Relief flooded me. "Yes, please."

"May I have your name?"

"Jane, Jane Delight."

The lady asked me to spell my surname. After I did, she scurried away, before returning moments later with a man who looked decidedly put out.

He was a little shorter than I was, with thick-rimmed glasses, and a slightly stooped, wearied air about him. His hair was dark with scarcely a touch of gray, although his manner gave me to believe he was older than he looked. "May I help you?" he asked.

"I'm helping Dr. Ramsgate," I told him.

"Oh yes, Reginald Ramsgate. How is he?"

I looked around, but the lady had returned to her seat and no other patrons were standing close by. "He's quite distressed, really. There was a murderer at the art gallery opening party the other night."

"There was? How terrible."

"You didn't hear about it?"

He shook his head. "I never watch the news. It's full of negativity."

I nodded slowly. "The police haven't solved the murder yet and apparently have no leads. Dr. Ramsgate is concerned that if they don't solve it soon, he'll have to cancel the opening of the next exhibition, and of course, that won't be good for the gallery."

"No, it wouldn't be good indeed, but I can't see how I can be of any assistance."

I added a little laugh. "It's quite a long story actually, but Dr. Ramsgate and I have been doing some sleuthing. Dr. Ramsgate seems to believe you have a sarcophagus in your Egyptian collection."

He rubbed his forehead with his left hand. "Yes, of course, Reginald knows that. We do have a sarcophagus from the Twenty-sixth Dynasty, and a much earlier one from the Third Intermediate Period. What could that possibly have to do with the murder?"

"Dr. Ramsgate believes the person has struck

before," I told him. I paused to draw breath. This wasn't the story I had wanted to use, and it was getting out of hand. What if this man called Dr. Ramsgate himself and found out everything I said was untrue? The man was looking at me expectantly, so I had no choice but to push on.

"Dr. Ramsgate said he was last here..." I hesitated and then said. "Oh goodness me, it's gone completely out of my mind. I forgot when he said he was here."

"Four years ago," he said. "He was here four years ago."

I smiled and nodded. "That's right. He said it was four or five years ago. He said it had something to do with the Egyptian artifacts."

Dr. Andersen leaned forward and peered at me.

I pushed on. "Dr. Ramsgate is dreadfully upset about the murder in the art gallery. Because it was at a public event, he has taken it personally and thinks someone is out to get him. The man who was murdered was over eighty, and Dr. Ramsgate is worried *he* was the target, that the other man was murdered by mistake."

"What do the police think?"

I shrugged. "They haven't made a comment on

that at all, which is why he is so worried."

"But what does this have to do with the artifacts?"

"Dr. Ramsgate was worried they might have been damaged in some way. He's concerned that the murderer has it in for him, for some reason." It sounded awfully lame to me, but apparently, he bought it.

Dr. Andersen gave a little shrug. "I'll show you around the museum, and then you can report to him that everything is okay."

I thanked him and followed him into his office. He retrieved a key, and I followed him down a long corridor. He unlocked the door and turned on the lights, and I followed him in. The room was definitely colder. I had expected it to be crammed with Egyptian artifacts, but there were hardly any.

Dr. Andersen gestured to a tiny item in a glass case. "This is a scarab from the early Eighteenth Dynasty." I didn't have my reading glasses on, so I squinted at the tiny item. "It depicts an ox."

"I see," I said.

"And this is the sarcophagus from the Third Intermediate Period."

My blood ran cold. Was the body of the real Dr. Ramsgate in that ancient coffin? The sarcophagus was in a glass case, but the other sarcophagus wasn't. "Why is this sarcophagus in a glass case, when this one's out in the open?" I asked him.

He shrugged. "Possibly, there wasn't enough funding for two glass cases. Maybe it is because this one is far more valuable. At any rate, it was Dr. Ramsgate's decision because he funded it."

"He didn't tell me that he funded it," I said, "and I didn't read about it in the papers."

Dr. Andersen nodded slowly. "Dr. Ramsgate is a very private person. He didn't want anyone to know of his generosity."

"Yes, he is very private indeed," I said. "So, he arranged this glass cabinet for the sarcophagus?"

Dr. Andersen nodded again. "Yes, it's a bit of an overkill, if you ask me, but still, I will never refuse funding." He chuckled to himself.

He walked along the small room showing me the other artifacts, a mummy's hand, several scarabs, and an amulet. "And over here we have a collection of shabtis," he concluded. "A shabti is a small funerary figure. Most of these were made from blue or green glazed faience, but we also have some in wood and clay."

"That's wonderful. Dr. Ramsgate will be thrilled everything is so safe," I told him.

He showed me out, but I don't remember anything else he said. My mind was in turmoil, and my stomach was churning.

One thing was clear—Dr. Ramsgate was certainly the Raven.

CHAPTER 20

*A*fter texting Matilda and Eleanor about what I had discovered, I drove home. I resisted the urge to stop at Rebecca's house to speak to Damon—I did not want him involved—and parked outside my gate.

Matilda and Eleanor had told me they would find their own way home in a further attempt to confuse the Raven. I certainly hoped it would work.

I parked outside my gate and grabbed a large handful of hay. I proceeded to walk toward my house, holding my hand out to the side, Billy trotting beside me and making horrible sounds as he munched greedily on the hay.

When I walked up the steps, I nearly tripped

over the potted plant Eleanor had put outside in the hopes of it catching some rain. The plant hadn't been doing well lately.

I looked at the plant and then slapped my palm on my forehead. How could I have been so silly! The potted plant in Dr. Ramsgate's office was half dead. His former secretary, Cindy Bellamy, had said he wanted to be a botanist and said that he loved plants. Surely, no plant lover would leave a plant in that condition.

That was a clue I had overlooked. It was one thing for me to overlook it, but why had Matilda and Eleanor overlooked it? They must have been slipping.

When I got home, I called Matilda and Eleanor, but it went straight to message bank in both cases. I looked out the window to see Billy trotting back to the front fence, no doubt to lie in wait for an unsuspecting victim.

Anxiety was gnawing away at me. I wouldn't rest until I had told Matilda and Eleanor what I had discovered. Of course, I had told them by text, but I wanted to tell them in person.

I was pacing up and down the living room when Mr. Crumbles appeared. I picked him up and tickled him under his chin. "I'm so bored that

I could take you outside and do some attack training with you," I told him with a laugh. "Only we would have to get past Billy."

"That goat wasn't really supposed to stop me, was he?" said a voice from the door.

My blood froze. My hair stood on end. I felt as though I had been given an electric shock. I turned around quickly, although it all seemed to happen in slow motion.

There, standing in the doorway, was Dr. Reginald Ramsgate, or should I say, the Raven.

"Have you hurt Billy?" I asked.

To my surprise, he appeared offended. "Of course not! I'm an animal lover. I was watching you with binoculars, and when I saw what you did to get to the house, I assumed the goat was vicious. I did exactly the same thing as you did with the hay, and look, I'm here safely. Where are your friends?"

"Who?"

He shot me another look. "The women known to you as Matilda and Eleanor."

"They're not home," I told him. I remembered that Matilda and Eleanor had counseled me to stick as close as possible to the truth, so I added, "I took Matilda to the mall, and I took Eleanor to the gym. They are going to make their own way home."

"I see. I heard you paid a little visit to Dr. Andersen."

I gasped. "How did you find out?"

"I paid Dr. Andersen a nice sum of money a few years ago to inform me if anybody ever asked for me, with a bonus if he ever had to alert me. You can imagine my surprise when he called me and told me you were asking questions. At least you didn't tell him that there are *two* bodies in that sarcophagus."

"Did you murder the man at the art gallery?"

He chuckled, a deep, menacing sound that sent a chill up my spine. "Jane, you and I both know that I did. I had given up trying to find Matilda and Eleanor, so I thought dispatching him at a public event might draw them out of the woodwork."

"Were you suspicious of them before that?" I asked, trying to keep him talking. My only hope was that Matilda and Eleanor would return home soon and save me.

"As a matter of fact, I wasn't," he admitted. "I moved here four years ago because I had a tipoff that they had been seen in the area, but before I got to my contact, he was killed in a rock-climbing accident. All I knew was that they were living in the general vicinity. I had no idea that they were sisters or even that they were living in close proximity to each other. I decided to move here and bide my time."

"But why did you assume someone else's identity?" I asked him. "Couldn't you have just made up a new identity?"

He looked down his long, pointed nose at me. "You know nothing about the spy business, obviously." His tone dripped with condescension.

I needed to keep the conversation going. "But why did you choose Dr. Ramsgate?"

"I did a fine arts degree at Oxford before I was tapped as a spy," he said. "I thought it would come in handy, and we were around the same age, height, and gender. I just had to grow a beard. And he was a loner with no friends or living relatives."

"So, Dr. Smythe isn't your daughter?"

He seemed genuinely surprised. "Dr. Smythe? No, of course not. Whatever gave you that idea?"

I shrugged. "But what about Silas Greeves? He wasn't your accomplice?"

"I always work alone." Again, the

condescending tone. He advanced a little toward me.

I took a step backward and picked up Mr. Crumbles. Mr. Crumbles proceeded to purr loudly.

If Matilda and Eleanor didn't come back quite soon, Mr. Crumbles was my only hope.

"What a shame your friends aren't here," he said. "I'll have to leave them a little message." He produced a large knife.

I gasped.

"I'm sure they'll be here soon," I said. "Why don't you wait for them?"

His eyes narrowed. "I'll leave them a little message first, and then I'll return to finish them off. It's more fun that way, you see."

I clutched Mr. Crumbles to me and backed away.

The Raven walked over to me, the knife raised.

I did my best to remember Eleanor's method of cat attack training, and I judged the distance. When the Raven was about five paces away, I gave Mr. Crumbles the preparation word, "Alert!"

The Raven stopped. "Excuse me?"

Mr. Crumbles looked up at me, his body tensed. I knew he was ready for action. "Face Hugger!" I yelled.

I threw Mr. Crumbles at the Raven's face.

Mr. Crumbles did superbly. In mid-air, he stuck out his claws and landed perfectly over the Raven's face, digging all his claws into his head.

The Raven screamed and dropped the knife, his arms flailing.

I hurried to retrieve the knife. Before I even reached it, Matilda and Eleanor appeared in the room. They were wearing flak jackets over their clothes, and Eleanor's hair was in rollers. Both were heavily armed.

Eleanor gave Mr. Crumbles the signal to release the Raven. I grabbed him and ran out of the room to the kitchen to reward him with cat treats. I didn't want to see what was happening in the other room.

There was a lot of noise, and presently Matilda put her head around the door. "You can come out now, Jane."

I picked up Mr. Crumbles and took him out. The Raven was sitting on a chair and was tied up very tightly indeed. There was a sock in his mouth. Blood oozed from the scratches on his face.

"We'll take him downstairs for interrogation soon," Matilda told me.

"When will you hand him over to the police?"

Both Matilda and Eleanor gasped. "No, we can't involve the police," Eleanor said. "This is an international espionage matter."

I crossed my arms over my chest. "You can't keep him downstairs forever."

Matilda chuckled. "Don't worry, Jane. We'll have him taken away."

"By whom?"

"We are not at liberty to divulge that," Eleanor said. "But you can't breathe a word of this to anybody. Dr. Ramsgate will simply go *missing*"—she made air quotes—"although we will anonymously inform the police that there are two bodies in that sarcophagus."

"He paid Dr. Andersen from the museum to tip him off if anybody asked questions," I said.

"Yes, we heard the whole conversation." Matilda smiled and nodded at me.

"What!" I shrieked. "You were listening in? All the time I thought I was going to die, and you were outside listening?"

"We were waiting for the right moment, of course," Matilda said happily.

Eleanor agreed. "And you *did* have Mr. Crumbles. He's the best attack cat in the business!"

The Raven made a horrible sound as though

he was trying to say something through the sock. I imagined his words weren't complimentary.

Something occurred to me. "Did the two of you suspect Dr. Ramsgate all along?"

The sisters exchanged glances and then nodded. "Yes, as soon as Cindy Bellamy said he wanted to be a botanist, I knew for sure," Matilda said.

"A botanist would never have a half-dead plant in his office," Eleanor added.

Now I was even more furious. "Why didn't you say something to me?"

"We didn't want to worry you," Matilda said as though it was the best excuse in the world. "After we take the Raven downstairs and lock him in the cell, let's all have some chocolate caramel cake to celebrate."

CHAPTER 21

I set my alarm for five in the morning, a time that should never have existed. I wanted to wake up early because Damon and I were having a picnic at noon, alone, with no crazy housemates or even crazier cats to disturb the peace. I wanted to wake up early because on this picnic with Damon—the picnic we were to have completely and entirely alone—I wanted to look ravishing. Pink, healthy cheeks. Hair windswept in the style of a Hollywood movie star. Teeth sparkling like diamonds in the golden sunlight. Damon would not know what hit him.

So, I needed time. I needed a lot of time. I needed to wax and pluck and polish and shine. I needed to watch several YouTube tutorials on how to do make-up for a lady of my age, with my wrinkles and my sun-damaged skin. I needed to pour myself into the dress I'd bought seven years ago and promised myself I would wear when I shed a few pounds. I had not shed a few pounds, but the color of the dress was magnificent, a deep purple, and it suited my skin. I was not a lady who spent a lot of money on clothes, so I really had no other option but this dress.

It took me all morning to get ready, but by the time Damon knocked on my door, I was ready to accept my rightful place as the diamond of the season.

"You look beautiful," Damon said as he kissed me on the cheek and blushed.

"Thank you," I said. I took care not to mention how much money I'd spent on make-up, hair serum, and shapewear. Actually, I was wearing three layers of shapewear, which meant I had zero mobility in my waist and had to walk stiffly along like a robot. I hoped I looked too magnificent for Damon to notice, but then he certainly was giving me a strange look as he escorted me to his shiny car.

I was happy Damon's right ankle was much better, that his car was not a stick shift, and that I did not need to drive. I felt so nervous about our picnic that I might swerve into the duck pond, which neither myself nor the ducks would enjoy.

We arrived ten minutes later at the pond, and I waited for Damon to look away before rolling from the car. I was so stiff in the shapewear I felt like a Barbie from the eighties—I had zero articulation. Still, I could not tell if I regretted the shapewear. Everything was pinched in wonderfully.

"I hope you like what I packed," Damon said as he took a picnic basket from the trunk of his car.

It turned out he had packed a wonderful picnic. He had really outdone himself. I had expected soggy tomato sandwiches slapped together in a rush, paper napkins, and bottles of lemonade that tasted more like sugar than lemons.

Instead, there was a cucumber salad dressed with sour cream on which a fillet of perfectly crisp salmon was perched. There were napkins, linen and embroidered. There was plenty of ice in which the champagne sat, cool and crisp, ready to be poured into our stemless glasses. Yes, Damon had packed stemless glasses.

"I called my mother in Scotland," he

explained, almost sheepishly. "I asked what kind of picnic would impress you."

Certainly, I felt very impressed indeed. However, I could not eat any of the food. Even the slightest slither of cucumber would cause me to burst out of my shapewear, perhaps sending the eleven glass buttons on my dress hurtling into the stratosphere and then back down to earth. No, I had not thought my three layers of shapewear through whatsoever.

"Everything is perfect," I said, truthfully.

Then I heard a car horn.

It was not like a regular car horn. It sounded like a novelty car horn, like a horn installed in a clown car. Damon and I both glanced over to the road, where we saw a perfectly normal car parked. The occupants of the car, however, were not perfectly normal, because the occupants of the car were Matilda and Eleanor.

Both stepped onto the grass, and both were wearing outfits like Sandy from *Grease*. Expect they were not dressed appropriately in the style of pre-makeover Sandy, in pastel skirts and charming little sweaters. No, they were dressed like post-makeover Sandy, in tight satin pants, red heels, and off-the-shoulder tops. Each had a leather jacket slung over one shoulder.

"What on earth," I said aloud. Damon nodded in agreement.

Frances stepped from the car. He was wearing a leather jacket with his name embroidered on the back, his hair slicked back in a greaser style, and dark sunglasses perched on his nose. He offered Matilda and Eleanor an arm each, and then the unholy trio strutted forward, clearly on the move to crash our romantic picnic.

"Should we just run?" I asked Damon.

"And leave the champagne? I bought it because I wanted to impress you."

"You *do* impress me," I replied, which made Damon blush even harder. There was something so charming about a grown man who acted like a shy schoolboy. I took his hand and smiled. We would both need a lot of strength to get through this picnic.

"This picnic looks like a real blast," Frances said.

"It sure does," Matilda replied.

My jaw dropped open. "What are you all doing?" I asked.

"What are *you* doing?" Frances countered.

"Er, Jane and I were having a romantic picnic," Damon replied. "You know, *alone*."

I looked behind them. "Wait, is that Mr. Crumbles?"

I had not noticed this before, but Mr. Crumbles was prowling behind Matilda, Eleanor, and Frances. I could hardly see how I might have missed him, given that he was also dressed in a black leather jacket.

"What have you done to poor Mr. Crumbles?" I said, jumping to my feet.

"He likes it," Matilda replied. "He's in our gang."

"You do not have a gang." I wanted to pull my hair out of my head.

"No," Eleanor said, "but we do have a lovely picnic spread. Damon, I can't believe you did all of this for us."

"Neither can I," Damon replied through gritted teeth.

Matilda, Eleanor, and Frances kicked off their shoes while I struggled to free Mr. Crumbles from his jacket. It turned out he did like it, because I had more than one scratch up my arm after our tussle had ended. Mr. Crumbles hissed at me and ran over to Damon, who scratched him behind the ear.

"Damon," Eleanor said, "may I offer you some cucumber salad?"

Damon looked too annoyed to speak.

"I suppose he isn't hungry," Matilda said. "More for us, I suppose."

Matilda, Eleanor, and Frances tucked into the picnic while Damon sat there, arms folded, glaring.

"Damon," I said gently, "perhaps we could go for a nice walk."

We left the picnic and walked toward the calming, still waters of the pond. I slipped my hand into Damon's, and soon I felt all the tension flood from his body. We could have a romantic picnic—only this romantic picnic would be without the picnic. I smiled at Damon as we stood by the water, and he smiled back. I knew for certain that nothing, not even Frances, could ruin this moment. That is when I heard the noise.

The patter of hooves.

The bleating.

Goats!

Matilda and Eleanor's goats were staring thoughtfully at the two of us. Relief surged through my body. When I heard the patter of hooves, I had feared the worst. I had feared Billy.

"Are they dangerous?" Damon asked. He sounded more than a little nervous.

"No," I assured him. "Not without their leader, Billy."

"You mean that Billy?" Damon pointed to a figure standing just behind the herd. It was Billy, and he looked angry.

"Run!" I cried.

"Run? Don't worry, Jane. I can handle a goat." Damon puffed out his chest, even though he sounded even more nervous than before.

I took his hand and sprinted toward the picnic. I did not have to look over my shoulder to know the herd of goats was stampeding after us. I could hear them.

"They are only little goats," Damon yelled as we ran. The poor man had no idea the dangerous situation we had all of a sudden found ourselves in.

Suddenly, Damon let go of my hand. I stopped running and glanced over my shoulder. Billy had jumped on Damon's back and was busily eating his hair. Soon, all of the goats swarmed around Damon like he was a breadcrumb and they were a nest of ants.

"Help me!" Damon yelled.

"You're on your own," I yelled back as I turned and ran. Damon was old enough to look after himself. He was strong and masculine and had the biggest arms of anyone I had ever seen. I, on the other hand, could not walk through life with goat-chewed hair.

I bolted straight past Matilda, Eleanor, and Frances, stopping briefly to scoop Mr. Crumbles into my arms. Soon, Mr. Crumbles and I found ourselves locked in Damon's car, our noses pressed against the glass, watching for any sign of goats.

We did not have to watch for long. The goat stampede appeared over the horizon and charged down on the romantic picnic. Matilda and Eleanor managed to flee in time, locking themselves in Frances's car. Only Frances was not so lucky.

The chaos lasted for a full fifteen minutes. The goats ate the cucumber salad. The goats ate the salmon. The goats ate the picnic blanket. I am sure the goats would have consumed all of the champagne too, if only they had known how to pop a cork. Silly goats.

After fifteen minutes, the stampede moved on, presumably in pursuit of their next victim. In their wake, they left a destroyed picnic and two very dazed men in desperate need of a hair stylist—or maybe a hair regrowth service. I was almost too afraid to unlock the car door when Damon tapped on the glass, his clothes in tatters, his hair chewed into strange and terrible shapes.

"I cannot believe you left me for dead," Damon said.

"You can handle yourself. I, on the other hand, am a delicate flower."

"Ha!" Damon said, and then he did the most surprising thing. He leaned over, and he kissed me, just once, on the nose. "Should we grab some pizzas and spend the afternoon watching television?"

"That sounds like my idea of a romantic picnic," I replied.

"Err," Damon added, "maybe we should lock the doors as soon as we get to your house. Just in case the goats come back."

"Great idea."

An hour later, Matilda, Eleanor, Frances, Damon, Mr. Crumbles, and I were all sitting in the living room. We did not mention missing chunks of hair. We did not mention cucumber salads. We did not mention goats. In fact, I am sure we did not mention anything at all. For a moment, I reflected on how nice it was to find people in the world who were just as weird and as magical as yourself. Damon threw his arm around me, and I smiled. I can't remember what television show we watched, only that it was a television show we all watched together, five strange humans, and one even stranger cat.

AMISH RECIPE

AMISH CHOCOLATE CARAMEL CAKE

INGREDIENTS
CAKE

2 cups all purpose flour

2 cups sugar

3/4 cups cocoa

2 eggs

2 teaspoons baking powder
1/2 cup oil
1 cup hot coffee
1 cup milk
pinch salt

INGREDIENTS
FROSTING

1/2 cup butter or butter substitute
1 cup brown sugar
1/4 cup chocolate milk
1/2 teaspoon vanilla extract
2 cups powdered sugar

METHOD
CAKE

Preheat oven to 350 degrees
Grease two 9 inch pans
Sift flour
Combine flour, sugar, cocoa, baking powder, salt
Make a well in the center and add oil, hot coffee, milk, lightly beaten eggs
Whisk gently until ingredients are combined.
Pour into two greased 9 inch pans

Bake approx. 30 minutes at 350 degrees

METHOD
FROSTING

Combine butter and brown sugar in a pan
Place over low heat
Add milk
Stir. When mixture comes to a boil, remove from heat
Allow to cool
When cool, add powdered sugar
Stir until frosting thickens

When cooled, spread frosting between the two layers and over entire outside of cake.

AMISH RECIPE

AMISH SOFT MOLASSES CUPCAKES

INGREDIENTS
CAKE

- 3 cups all purpose flour
- 1 cup packed brown sugar
- 1/4 teaspoon salt
- 1 cup vegetable oil
- 3 teaspoons baking soda

AMISH RECIPE

2 eggs
1 cups boiling water
1 cup molasses

METHOD
CAKE

Preheat oven to 350°.
Line muffin pan with paper liners, or grease pan.
In a large bowl, combine oil, sugar, molasses and lightly-beaten eggs.
Whisk in flour and salt.
Combine boiling water and baking soda. Add to mixture, lightly combine.
Spoon into pan, filling each two-thirds full.
Bake for 16-20 minutes until the cakes rebound when lightly touched with finger or when an inserted toothpick comes out clean.
Cool on cooling rack.
When cool, spread on frosting.

INGREDIENTS
FROSTING

1 lb cream cheese (packaged)
1/2 cup butter

1/4 cup molasses
1 teaspoon vanilla extract
8 cups powdered sugar

INGEDIENTS
CAKE

In a mixing bowl, beat cream cheese with butter . Combine with molasses and vanilla. Beat on low until well combined.

Slowly add little powdered sugar at a time.

ABOUT RUTH HARTZLER

USA Today Best-selling author Ruth Hartzler spends her days writing, walking her dog, and thinking of ways to murder somebody. That's because Ruth writes mysteries and adventures.

She is best known for her archeological adventures, for which she relies upon her former career as a college professor of ancient languages and Biblical history.

www.ruthhartzler.com

Made in the USA
Monee, IL
12 October 2021